HARLEQUIN®
Presents~

Take time out from your busy schedule this month to
kick back and relax with a brand-new Harlequin Presents
novel. We hope you enjoy this month's selection.

If you love royal heroes, you're in for a treat this month!
In Penny Jordan's latest book, *The Italian Duke's Wife*,
an Italian aristocrat chooses a young English woman
as his convenient wife. When he unleashes within
her a desire she never knew she possessed, he is soon
regretting his no-consummation rule.... Emma Darcy's
sheikh in *Traded to the Sheikh* is an equally powerful
and sexy alpha male. This story has a wonderfully exotic
desert setting, too!

We have some gorgeous European men this month.
Shackled by Diamonds by Julia James is part of our
popular miniseries GREEK TYCOONS. Read about a
Greek tycoon and the revenge he plans to exact on an
innocent, beautiful model when he wrongly suspects
her of stealing his priceless diamonds. In Sarah Morgan's
Public Wife, Private Mistress, can a passionate Italian's
marriage be rekindled when he is unexpectedly reunited
with his estranged wife?

In *The Antonides Marriage Deal* by Anne McAllister, a
Greek magnate meets a stunning new business partner,
and he begins to wonder if he can turn their business
arrangement into a permanent contract—such as
marriage! Kay Thorpe's *Bought by a Billionaire* tells of
a Portuguese billionaire and his ex-lover. He wants her
back as his mistress. Previously she rejected his proposal
because of his arrogance and his powerful sexuality. But
this time he wants marriage....

Happy reading! Look out for a brand-new selection next
month.

Models & Millionaire$

*She's divinely beautiful and
pursued by a millionaire!*

Escape to a world of absolute wealth and
glamour in this brand-new duet from Julia James.
These models find themselves surrounded by
beauty and sophistication. It can be a false
world, but fortunately there are strong alpha
millionaires waiting in the wings to claim them!

**Look out for part two of this
glamorous duet, coming in May 2006**

For Pleasure...Or Marriage?
by Julia James
#2536

Julia James

SHACKLED BY DIAMONDS

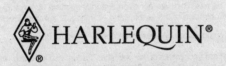

TORONTO • NEW YORK • LONDON
AMSTERDAM • PARIS • SYDNEY • HAMBURG
STOCKHOLM • ATHENS • TOKYO • MILAN • MADRID
PRAGUE • WARSAW • BUDAPEST • AUCKLAND

If you purchased this book without a cover you should be aware
that this book is stolen property. It was reported as "unsold and
destroyed" to the publisher, and neither the author nor the
publisher has received any payment for this "stripped book."

ISBN 0-373-12531-3

SHACKLED BY DIAMONDS

First North American Publication 2006.

Copyright © 2006 by Julia James.

All rights reserved. Except for use in any review, the reproduction or
utilization of this work in whole or in part in any form by any electronic,
mechanical or other means, now known or hereafter invented, including
xerography, photocopying and recording, or in any information storage
or retrieval system, is forbidden without the written permission of the
publisher, Harlequin Enterprises Limited, 225 Duncan Mill Road,
Don Mills, Ontario, Canada M3B 3K9.

All characters in this book have no existence outside the imagination of the
author and have no relation whatsoever to anyone bearing the same
name or names. They are not even distantly inspired by any individual
known or unknown to the author, and all incidents are pure invention.

This edition published by arrangement with Harlequin Books S.A.

® and TM are trademarks of the publisher. Trademarks indicated with
® are registered in the United States Patent and Trademark Office, the
Canadian Trade Marks Office and in other countries.

www.eHarlequin.com

Printed in U.S.A.

All about the author...
Julia James

JULIA JAMES lives in England with her family. Harlequin® novels were the first "grown-up" books Julia read as a teenager, and she's been reading them ever since.

Julia adores the English countryside (and the Celtic countryside!) in all its seasons, and is fascinated by all things historical, from castles to cottages. She also has a special love for the Mediterranean. She considers both ideal settings for romance stories! Since becoming a romance writer, she has, she says, had the great good fortune to start discovering the Caribbean as well, and is happy to report that those magical, beautiful islands are also ideal settings for romance stories! "One of the best things about writing romance is that it gives you a great excuse to take vacations in fabulous places!" says Julia. "And all in the name of research, of course!"

Her first stab at novel writing was Regency romances. "But alas, no one wanted to publish them!" she says. She put her writing aside until her family commitments were clear, and then renewed her love affair with contemporary romances to great success.

In between writing, Julia enjoys walking, gardening, needlework and baking "extremely gooey chocolate cakes"—and trying to stay fit!

CHAPTER ONE

LEO MAKARIOS paused in the shadows at the top of the flight of wide stairs leading down to the vast hall of Schloss Edelstein, one hand curved around the newel post of the massive carved wood banister, his powerful physique relaxing as he surveyed the arc-lit scene below with a sense of satisfaction.

Justin had chosen well. The four girls really were exquisite.

He stood a moment, looking them over.

The blonde caught his eye first, but despite her remarkable beauty she was too thin for his tastes, her pose too tense. He had no patience with neurotic women. The brunette beside her wasn't too thin, but for all her glorious swathe of chestnut hair her expression was vacant. Leo's gaze moved on. Unintelligent women irritated him.

The redhead's pre-Raphaelite looks were stunning indeed, but they had, Leo knew, already caught the attention of his cousin Markos, under whose protection the girl was living. His gaze moved on again to the final girl.

And stopped.

His eyes narrowed, taking in the picture she made.

The hair was sable. As black as night.

The skin was white. As pale as ivory.

And the eyes were green.

As green as the emeralds she was wearing.

Wearing with an air of such total boredom that a sudden shaft of anger went through him. What business had any female to look *bored* when wearing a Levantsky necklace? Did she not realise what a miracle of the jeweller's art the necklace was? And the earrings and the bracelets and the rings she was adorned with?

Evidently not. Even as he watched her lips pressed together

and she gave a conspicuously heavy sigh, placing one hand on her hip and very obviously shifting her weight from one leg to the' other beneath her long skirts.

Leo stilled, the anger draining out of him. As she'd given that heavy sigh her breasts had lifted. Already lush from the tightly corseted black gown she was wearing, the movement had made their soft dove-white mounds swell delectably.

Through Leo's lean, powerful frame a familiar and pleasurable sensation started.

So the sable-haired, green-eyed beauty was bored, was she?

Well, he would be happy to remedy that.

Personally.

He started to walk down the stairs.

Anna felt her mood worsening. What was the hold-up now? Tonio Embrutti had gone into a huddle with his assistants, and she could hear the static hiss of vituperative Italian. She gave another sigh, feeling the low-cut décolletage digging in. She hated wearing it—it was far too revealing, and it invited the usual sleazy male attention she tried to avoid.

Her lips pressed together again. Mentally she forced herself to go through one of her karate *katas*. It both calmed her and reassured her, knowing she could fight off any physical harassment—even if she couldn't stop men leering over her.

She shifted her weight again minutely in the heavy dress. Modelling wasn't as easy as people thought it was, and she could tell that the two amateurs here—Kate and Vanessa—were finding it hard and tiring. Anna's eyes travelled to them. The brunette, Kate, looked vacant without her lenses in—but at least, thought Anna, it meant she couldn't see the lecherous looks aimed at her. The redhead, Vanessa, had other protection—word had gone round that her boyfriend was the cousin of the guy who'd set up this shindig and owned this medieval mansion. Though why, Anna mused, a Greek should own a castle in the Austrian Alps was beyond her. Maybe he just wanted to be close to the private Swiss bank he kept his loot in.

He certainly had a whole load of cash, that was for sure. Schloss Edelstein was vast, perched halfway up a mountain and surrounded by forests and snowfields.

Anna's bored expression lightened suddenly with remembered pleasure. The view from her bedroom was breathtaking: sunlight sparkling on the pristine snow, down to the frozen lake below, ringed by mountains. Very different from the view of the gasworks she'd had when she was growing up.

But then Anna had been lucky, she knew—spectacularly lucky.

Spotted in a shopping mall when she was eighteen by a scout for a modelling agency, she'd been incredibly suspicious at first. But the offer had proved genuine. Not that it hadn't taken non-stop hard work to succeed at modelling. Now, even though she was not in the supermodel bracket, and at twenty-six was already facing up to her limited remaining shelf-life, she made a living that was light-years away from what she'd been born to.

She'd learned a lot along the way. Not just how the other half lived—which had opened her eyes big-time—but about how to survive in one of the toughest careers around. And do it without letting the slime get to you.

Because slime, she had swiftly discovered, was a big, big feature of a fashion model's world. Some of the girls, she knew, did every drug they could, and slept with every man who could help their career. And a lot of the men in the fashion world weren't any better either.

Not that everyone was like that, she acknowledged. Some people in the fashion world were fine—there were designers she respected, photographers she trusted, models who were friends. Like Jenny, the blonde of the quartet, her best friend, draped now in white, with a diamond tiara and bracelets up to her elbows.

Anna's eyes narrowed.

Jenny didn't look well. She'd always been thin—what model wasn't?—but now she was on the point of looking emaciated. It wasn't drugs—Jenny didn't do drugs, or Anna would not have been friends with her. She hoped it wasn't just under-eating—especially not if some jerk of a photographer had been telling her to shift some non-existent weight. Illness? A shudder went through Anna. Life was uncertain enough, and you could die in your twenties all right. Hadn't her own mother not made it past twenty-five, leaving her fatherless baby daughter to be brought up by her widowed grandmother?

Whatever it was that was pulling Jenny down, Anna would try and catch some time with her, when today's shoot had finished. If it ever did. At least the huddle around Tonio Embrutti seemed to be ending. He was turning his attention back to the models. His little eyes flashed in his fleshy face, which a cultivated designer stubble did not enhance.

'You!' He pointed dramatically at Jenny. 'Off!'

Anna saw Jenny stare.

'Off?' she echoed dumbly.

The photographer waved his hands irritably.

'The dress. Off. Down to the hips. Peel it off. Then I need the hands crossed over in your cleavage. I want to shoot the bracelets. Hurry up!' He clicked impatiently at a hovering stylist and held out a hand for his camera from his assistant.

Jenny stood frozen.

'I can't.'

The photographer stared at her.

'Are you deaf? Remove your dress. Now!'

The stylist he'd pointed at was obediently undoing the fastenings down the back of Jenny's dress.

'I'm not taking the dress off!'

Jenny's voice sounded high-pitched with tension.

Anna saw Tonio Embrutti's face darken. She stepped forward to intervene.

'No strips,' she announced. 'It's in the contract.'

The photographer's face whipped round to hers.

'Shut up!' He turned back to Jenny.

Anna walked up to her, putting a hand out to stop the stylist. Jenny was looking as tense as a board.

Another voice spoke. A new voice.

'Do we have a problem?'

The voice was deep, and accented. It was also—and Anna could hear it like a low, subliminal tremor in her body—a warning.

A man had stepped out of the shadows consuming the rest of the vast hall beyond the brilliantly illuminated space they were being photographed in.

Anna felt the breath catch in her throat. The man who had stepped into the circle of light was like a leopard. Sleek, powerful, graceful—and dangerous.

Dangerous? She wondered why the word had come into her mind, but it had. And even as it formed it was replaced by another one.

Devastating.

The breath stayed caught in her throat as she stared, taking in everything about the man who had just appeared.

Tall. Very tall. Taller than her.

Dark hair, olive skin—and a face that could have stepped out of a Byzantine mosaic. Impassive, remote, assessing.

And incredibly sexy.

It was the eyes, she thought, as she slowly exhaled her breath. The eyes that did it. Almond-shaped, heavy-lidded, sensual.

Very dark.

He spoke again. Everyone seemed to have gone totally silent around him. He was the kind of man who'd have that effect on people, Anna found herself thinking.

'I repeat—do we have a problem?'

He doesn't like problems—he gets rid of them. They get in his way…

The words seemed to form in her mind of their own accord.

'And you are…?' Tonio Embrutti enquired aggressively.

Stupidly.

The man turned his impassive heavy-lidded eyes on him. For a moment he said nothing.

'Leo Makarios,' he said.

He didn't say it loudly, thought Anna. He didn't say it portentously. And he certainly didn't say it self-importantly.

Yet there was something about the way the man who owned Schloss Edelstein, whose company owned every jewel that she and the other three models were draped with, and who owned a whole heap more besides spoke. Something about the way he said his name that almost—almost—made her feel sorry for Tonio Embrutti.

Almost, but not quite. Because Tonio Embrutti was, without doubt, one of the biggest jerks she'd ever had the displeasure to be photographed by.

'Yes,' she announced clearly, before the photographer could get a word out. 'We do have a problem.'

The heavy-lidded eyes turned to her.

How, she found herself thinking, could eyes that were so impassive make her feel every muscle in her body tighten? As though she were an impala—caught out on a deserted African plain, with the sun going down.

When the big cats came out to hunt.

But she wasn't an impala, and this Leo Makarios was no leopard. He was just a rich man who was having a fun time getting his latest rich-man's toy some media attention. Starting with publicity photos, courtesy of four models specially hired for the purpose.

But *not* hired to strip.

'Your photographer,' she said sweetly, 'wants us to breach the contract.' Her voice changed. Hardened. 'No nude work. It's in the contract,' she informed him. 'I made sure it was. Check it out.'

She went on standing protectively beside Jenny. The other two girls—the amateurs—had, she noticed, instinctively closed in on each other as well. Both were looking uneasy.

Leo Makarios was still looking at her.

She was looking back.

Something was happening to her.

Something deep down. In her guts.

Something she didn't like.

Slime. Was that it? Was that what it was about the way Leo Makarios was looking at her that she didn't like?

No, she thought slowly. Definitely not slime. That she could handle. She'd had to learn how, and now she could.

But this was worse. What Leo Makarios was doing to her hit somewhere completely different.

She could feel it happening. Feel the slow, heavy slug of her heart rate. Feel the blood start to pulse.

As if for the very first time in her life.

Oh, no, she thought, with the kind of slow-motion thinking that came with great shock. Not this.

Not him.

But it was.

Leo let his eyes rest on her.

She wasn't looking bored now.

Two quite different emotions were animating her face, though she was, he could see, trying not to let the second one through.

The first emotion was anger. The girl was angry. Very angry.

It was an old anger too, one that was familiar to her.

But the second emotion was coming as a shock to her.

He felt a surge of satisfaction go through him.

She might be hiding it, but he'd seen it—seen the tell-tale minute flaring of her pupils as her eyes had impacted with his.

The satisfaction came again, but he put it to one side. He'd attend to it later—when the time was appropriate. Right now he had other matters to deal with.

He flicked his eyes to the blonde. Yes, definitely the neurotic type, he thought. Tense and jittery, and the type to give any man a headache. She was fantastically beautiful, of course, but he didn't envy the man who had the handling of her.

'Let me understand,' he said to her. 'You do not want this shot? The one Signor Embrutti desires?'

The girl was almost trembling she was so tense. She shook her head.

Tonio Embrutti burst into a fusillade of staccato Italian. Leo halted him with a peremptory hand.

'No breast shots. Not for her. Not for any of them. Their clothes stay on—all of them,' he spelt out, for good measure.

His eyes moved over the four girls, resting momentarily on the redhead. A smile almost flickered on his mouth. He could just imagine his cousin Markos's reaction to seeing his mistress's naked charms paraded in the publicity shots accompanying the launch of the rediscovered Levantsky collection—long-hidden in a secret Tsarist cache in the depths of Siberia and recently returned to the commercial world courtesy of a shrewd acquisition by Makarios Corp.

Markos would have beaten him to a pulp for allowing it!

If he could land a punch, that was, thought Leo, with dark humour.

Not that he would give him cause to—or any man who had an interest in the girls here.

His eyes flicked back to the sable-haired model. Was she taken? Just because she'd responded to him it didn't mean that another man didn't have his marker on her. She wouldn't be the first female to think she'd do better trading up to a Makarios.

Those that thought that way, however, he promptly lost interest in.

Such women made poor mistresses. Their minds were on his money—not on him.

And when he had a woman in bed with him he wanted her mind totally and utterly on him.

As the sable-haired model's would be when he bedded her. He would see to it.

He strolled to the side of the vast hall, nodding briefly to the senior security personnel hired to guard the Levantsky collection, leaned back against the edge of a heavy oak table, crossed one ankle over the other, folded his arms, and watched, wanting to see more of the girl he had selected for himself.

The shoot went on.

It was the turn of the sable-haired model next. Both to be shot and picked on.

Tonio Embrutti was clearly taking out his spleen on her. Nothing she did was right. He snapped and snarled and sneered at whatever she did, however she posed.

Leo felt an intense desire to stride across to the photographer and wring his scrawny neck. And he also felt a grudging admiration for the model.

She might be bored wearing a Levantsky *parure*, she might be the kind of troublemaker who quoted contractual conditions at the first sign of rough water, but when it came to putting up with what was being handed out to her she had the patience of a saint.

Which was curious, thought Leo, watching her assessingly, because she didn't look saint-like at all.

Not that she looked sexy.

Nothing that crass.

No, her intense sexual allure came from something quite different.

It came from her being supremely indifferent to it.

It really was, he mused, very powerful.

Very erotic.

His eyes swept over her. The black hair like a cloak, the milk-white shoulders and generous curve of her corseted breasts, her tiny waist and her accentuated hips, her slender but moulded arms—and then her face, of course. Almost square, with a defined jaw, and yet the high cheekbones, the straight nose, the wide, unconsciously voluptuous mouth—and the emerald eyes...

Oh, yes, she really was very, very erotic.

He felt his body stir, and he relaxed back to enjoy the view.

And anticipate the night's entertainment to come.

Courtesy of the sable-haired model.

Idly, he wondered what her name was...

Anna sank her exhausted body into the hot, fragrant water. It felt blissful. God, she was tired. The shoot had been punishing.

Not just because of that jerk Embrutti—though keeping her cool with him had taken more effort than she enjoyed exerting—but simply because it had taken so long.

But in the end it had been a wrap. Every girl had been photographed wearing every different colour stone, with both matching and contrasting gowns. They would be wearing the jewels again tonight, at the grand reception Leo Makarios was holding to launch his revival of the Levantsky jewellery marque. Vanessa in emeralds, Kate in rubies, herself in diamonds and Jenny in sapphires.

Anna's eyes were troubled suddenly. She'd had her little chat with Jenny, following her into her room when they'd all finally been dismissed. She'd plonked her down on the bed, sat down beside her, and got the truth from her.

And it had shocked her totally.

'I'm pregnant!' Jenny had blurted out.

Anna had just stared. She hadn't needed to ask who by, or just why Jenny was so upset about it.

She'd warned her all along not to get involved with someone whose culture was so different from Western norms, that it could only end in trouble.

And it certainly had.

'He told me!' Jenny had rocked back and forth on the bed, clutching her abdomen where, scarcely visible, her baby was growing. 'He told me that if ever I got pregnant I faced two choices. Marrying him and living as his wife to raise the child. Or marrying him, giving him the child, and being divorced. But I can't. I can't do either! I can't!'

She'd started crying, and Anna had wrapped her up in her arms and let her cry.

'I can't marry him!' Jenny had sobbed. 'I can't live in some harem and never get out ever again. And as for giving up my baby…'

Her sobs had become even more anguished.

'I take it,' Anna had said, when they finally died away, 'that he doesn't know about the baby?'

'No! And he mustn't find out! Or he'll come and get me and

drag me back to his desert. Oh, God, Anna, he mustn't find out. Don't you see why I was so terrified when Tonio wanted me to strip down? In case it showed—the pregnancy. Supposing someone noticed—they would; you know they would—and it started circulating as a rumour. He'd pick up on it and he'd come storming down on me! Oh, God, I've got to get away. I've got to.'

Anna had frowned.

'Get away?'

'Yes. I've got to hide. Hide before anything starts really showing. And I mean hide for good, Anna. If he ever hears I've had a baby he'll know it's his. He'll have tests done and all that. So I've got to get away.'

She'd turned a stricken face to her friend.

'I've got to get really, really far away—and stay there. Totally resettle. Somewhere he'll never think of looking.' She bit her lip. 'I was planning on Australia. One of the obscure bits, round the northwest. Where the pearls come from. I can't remember what it's called, but it's the last place he'd look.'

Anna had looked sober.

'Can you afford to move out there, Jenny?'

She knew Jenny earned good money, but it was patchy. Neither of them were in the very top league of supermodels, and agency fees and other expenses ate into what they were paid. Besides, Jenny's ill-advised affair with the man she was now desperate to flee from had kept her out of circulation for too long—other, younger models were snapping up work she'd have now been grateful to get.

Jenny hadn't answered. Just bitten her lip.

'I can lend you—' Anna began, but Jenny had shaken her head.

'You need your money. I know how expensive that nursing home is for your gran. And I won't have you selling your flat. At our age we're both looking extinction in the face—you need your savings for when you quit modelling. So I'm not borrowing from you. I'll manage. Somehow.'

Anna hadn't bothered to press her offer. Somehow she

would make sure Jenny had at least enough to start running, start hiding—even if it meant mortgaging her flat to raise some cash.

Now she lay back in the water, letting the heat drain her tiredness. Poor Jenny—pregnant by a man who valued her only as a body, and who would part her from her baby with the click of his imperious fingers. Neither of the generous 'options' he'd given her was acceptable. No, Jenny had to get away, all right. As soon as this shoot was over.

But there was more to get through yet. Already guests had started to arrive. Driven up in chauffeured cars or deposited via helicopter. The rich, the famous, the influential—all invited by Leo Makarios.

She stared at the steam gently rising from the huge claw-footed bathtub.

Leo Makarios.

She was going to have to think about him.

She didn't want to.

Had been putting it off.

But now she had to think about him.

Cautiously she opened her mind to what had happened.

For the first time in four long, safe years she had seen a man who was dangerous to her.

And it was disturbing.

Because men weren't dangerous to her. Not any more. Not since Rupert Vane had told her that he was off to marry Caroline Finch-Carleton—a girl, unlike Anna, from his own upper-crust background.

Even now, four years on, she could still feel the burn of humiliation. Of hurt.

Rupert had been the first man—the only man—who had got past her defences. He'd had the lazily confident good-mannered charm of a scion of the landed classes, and he'd simply breezed through each and every one of her rigidly erected guards. He had been funny, and fun, and fond of her in his own shallow way.

'It's been a hoot, Anna,' he'd told her as he'd given her the news about his forthcoming marriage.

Since then she'd kept men—all men—at a safe distance. Thanking heaven, in a perverse way, that most of the ones she encountered held no attraction for her.

Into her mind, as the water lapped her breasts, an image stole. A picture of a man looking her over with dark heavy-lidded eyes.

Leo Makarios.

Deliberately she let herself think about him. I need to know, she thought. I need to know why he's dangerous to me.

So that I can guard against it.

Something had happened today that had got her worried. A man had looked her over and it had got to her. And she didn't know why.

It couldn't be because he was good looking—her world was awash with fantastic-looking men, and not all of them were gay. And it couldn't be because he was rich—because that had always been the biggest turn-off, accompanied as it usually was by an assumption that models were sexually available to rich men.

So what the hell was going on?

All she knew were two things.

That when it came to Leo Makarios she would have to be very, very careful.

And that she wanted to see him again.

CHAPTER TWO

EFFORTLESSLY, Leo switched from Italian to French, and then into German and English, as he greeted his guests. The vast hall had been cleared of all the photographic clutter, and was now thronged with women in evening dress and men in black tie, and waiters circulating with trays of champagne.

'Markos!' Leo switched to Greek and greeted his cousin. A couple of years younger than Leo's thirty-four, and of slightly slimmer build, his dark slate eyes revealed his portion of English ancestry. Markos was otherwise all Greek. They chatted a moment or two, and Leo cast a courteous smile at the pre-Raphaelite redhead at Markos's side.

She didn't return the smile. She didn't even see him. She was gazing at his cousin with a bemused, helpless expression in her eyes, as though Markos were the only person in the universe.

A strange ripple of emotion went through Leo.

No woman had ever looked at him like that...

Would you want them to?

The question thrust rhetorically, challengingly.

He answered promptly.

No, definitely not. Any woman who looked at him like that would be a nuisance.

Or faking it.

In the past there had been women who'd passionately declared their undying love for him, but he'd known better. The object of their devotion was not him, but his wealth. Now he never let any woman tell him she loved him.

He made the terms of his endearment crystal-clear from the outset. A temporary affair, exclusive while it lasted, with no emotional scenes to irritate him, no hysterical recriminations when it came to an end, and no post-affair harassment. When it was over, it was over—and could they please both move on? He would—she must too. They would inevitably cross paths again in the cosmopolitan world he moved in, and he didn't want any unwelcome scenes or unpleasant encounters.

He moved through the throng, meeting and greeting his myriad guests. His eyes were scanning the crowd, picking out the models circulating with their display of Levantsky jewels.

Where was the sable-haired one?

Suddenly he saw her, and he stopped dead.

She looked absolutely and totally stunning.

She was wearing a black dress so simple it was almost a sarong, wrapped tightly across her breasts and then falling in a single fluid line to her ankles. With it she wore black elbow-length evening gloves. Unlike earlier, her hair was up, in a soft, immensely flattering low pompadour on the back of her head, framing her face. She had far less make-up on than she'd had for the shoot; her mouth merely seemed to have lipgloss, and her eyes little more than mascara. Her skin was still ivory-white.

Against the whiteness the shimmer of diamonds circling her slender throat glittered iridescently, enhancing her already exquisite beauty.

For a full moment Leo did nothing but look, taking in the vision she presented. She really was quite exceptional...

Then, abruptly, a frown drew his brows together. He strode towards her.

She'd been standing on her own, a glass of champagne in one long black-satined hand, and she was gazing up at the snarling mask of a long-dead boar on one of the walls. There was an expression of strong disapproval on her face.

'Why are you not wearing the rest of the *parure*?' he demanded as he reached her.

Her head spun round.

There was that flaring of her pupils again, he could see it. But right now he wasn't interested. He was interested only in why she was not wearing the tiara, earrings and bracelets that matched the necklace, as she'd been instructed to do that evening.

'Well?' he prompted.

She seemed to collect herself minutely.

'One of the bulbs was on the blink,' she answered.

Leo frowned more deeply.

'What?' he snapped.

'As in Christmas lights. I mean,' she asked him, 'did you actually want me wandering around looking like a Christmas tree? It just looked ridiculously overdone wearing the whole lot together.'

'And that was your decision, was it?'

The tone was mild, but it raised the hairs on the back of Anna's neck.

There was no way she was backing down, though. She'd seen her reflection when she'd been wearing the whole lot, and she'd just looked like a glitterball.

'It would,' she riposted pointedly, 'be the decision of anyone who had any taste.'

His eyes narrowed at her tone. 'My instructions were quite clear.'

Anna knew exactly what she should say. Leo Makarios was paying her to model his jewellery, and he called the shots. She should say docilely, *Of course, Mr Makarios. Three bags full, Mr Makarios.*

But she didn't.

'Well, you were wrong,' she said instead. 'To wear any more jewellery than this necklace would be irredeemably vulgar.'

His face stilled. Something changed in the heavy-lidded eyes. She ought to back down; she knew she should. But she never backed down. If you did you got walked over.

For one long moment his eyes simply rested on her. She could feel the tension start to edge through her.

Then she realised what he was doing.

Out-psyching her.

So she took the battle into his corner.

'Surely, Mr Makarios,' she posed limpidly, 'a man with all your money would not wish to appear vulgar?'

For one timeless second it hung in the balance. And for that moment Anna found herself hoping for something—and she didn't even know why she was hoping for it.

But she got it all the same.

At the corner of his mouth, almost imperceptibly, she saw a quirk.

Something lightened inside her. She didn't know what, or why, but it did.

Then the quirk vanished and the mouth was a straight, tight line once more, the heavy-lidded eyes quelling.

'You live dangerously,' said Leo Makarios softly. 'Don't do it on my time.'

He gave a brief indication of his head. 'Go and put the jewels back on.'

He walked away. Cutting her out of existence.

For one intense moment an urge so strong almost overpowered her and she had to steel her whole body. She wanted to vault forward, lift her empty hand up and bring it slashing down. But, slowly, she stood, letting the aggressive urge drain out of her. Why on earth should she let a man like Leo Makarios get to her? He was just one more rich man who liked the world the way he paid it to be. And right now he was paying her to wear his jewels. All his jewels. However vulgar such an over-the-top display would be. She gave a shrug.

He wanted diamonds? She'd put on diamonds.

As she strode off, as fast as her narrow skirt would permit, she did not see a pair of heavy-lidded eyes flick past the shoulder of the chief executive Leo happened to be speaking to and rest narrowingly on her.

Then, as she disappeared from view, he went back seamlessly to discussing the implications of the latest G8 summit on world trade.

The chamber orchestra was tuning up, people were taking their seats in the ballroom. Unlike the medieval-style hall, the ball-

room was pure rococo, lined with mirrors and with an extrav-
agantly carved gilded ceiling. Set diagonally, like miniature
wings either side of the orchestra, were two pairs of gilt *fau-
teuils*. They were for the models, so the audience could admire
the Levantsky jewels in their massed splendour while they lis-
tened to Mozart. Three of the girls, noted Leo, as he entered,
had just taken their places. His eyes flicked over them again
as he made some conversational reply to the wife of one of the
Austrian government ministers sitting beside him.

The redhead was gazing into the audience, openly searching
for Markos. The brunette, Leo noted with mild surprise, had
lost her vacant look and was talking animatedly to the musician
closest to her.

His eyes flicked across to the two chairs on the other side
of the orchestra. The blonde was there, looking more uptight
than ever, but the chair beside her was empty.

Leo felt his mouth tightening again.

Definitely a troublemaker.

He'd had confirmation. He'd sent for his aide, Justin, who
was taking care of the publicity side of the Levantsky launch,
and told him to check that the black-haired girl was this time
obeying orders. Justin had looked nervous, and muttered something about her agency warning him that she had a bit of an
attitude issue.

Leo had just looked at Justin. 'Not while she's here,' he'd
said.

Justin had scurried off.

Leo took his place beside the minister's wife. The orchestra
went on tuning up.

The girl cut it fine. Very fine.

The audience were finally quietening; the conductor was at
his podium.

She came gliding in, whisking into her seat. Then she just
sat there, hands folded demurely in her lap.

She had the tiara in her hair, long drops in her ears, bracelets
on both arms, and the necklace of diamonds.

Looking exactly like an illuminated Christmas tree.

Leo's mouth tightened.

He hated being wrong. About anything.

Or anyone.

Anna's feet were killing her again. It was the worst aspect of modelling, she thought—apart from the boredom and the sleaze.

But she stood, politely attentive, while a stout German industrialist regaled her with the healing properties of spa waters. Across the room, Anna could see Leo Makarios talking to someone. She hoped he was happy with the Christmas lights.

They were certainly getting enough attention from the guests, that was for sure. She'd been on the receiving end of countless inspections by both men and women—though the male ones had been liberally blended with lecherous looks as well—speculating about the price. And not just of the jewels.

That was why she was sticking where she was. Spa cures might not be the most fascinating subject in the world, but the German industrialist was treating her with great courtesy. Better still, he was keeping other men away from her.

All except one.

'Hans, *wie gehts*?'

The deep, accented voice was unmistakable.

Anna felt herself tense automatically, vivid with awareness of who had just approached.

The industrialist's face lit into a warm smile and he launched into German. As Leo Makarios answered him in the same language, his voice rich and smooth, Anna could feel him looking at her, taking in the ostentatious display of diamonds she was showing off.

As he regarded her she kept her face expressionless, her eyes blank.

For a moment Leo thought of telling her that she'd been right, that wearing the entire *parure* was overkill, detracting from the exquisite beauty of the rainfall necklace.

Then Hans Federman was asking a question about his experience of doing business in the former Eastern Bloc, and comparing it with his own company's experiences.

Taking advantage of the diversion, Anna was about to drift off. But as she started to move, without pausing a beat in what he was saying, Leo Makarios snaked his hand out and fastened it round her wrist.

Anna froze. Entirely opposite reactions flashed through her. One was an instinct to yank her arm away from his restraining hold. The second was a bolt of hot electricity that shocked her to her core.

Then, abruptly, her wrist was dropped. Leo Makarios stopped talking and turned his head to her.

'Don't wander off, please, Ms…?' He cocked an eyebrow at her, pointedly waiting for her to supply her name.

'Anna Delane,' she said reluctantly. She wondered why she was so unwilling to let Leo Makarios know her name. All he had to do was ask one of his scores of minions, including that obsequious toady Justin Vennor, who'd lectured the four models for half an hour on how they must behave impeccably in such august and glittering surroundings.

'Anna.'

It was just her name, that was all. She'd heard it said all her life.

But not like this…

A shiver went down her spine. She could feel it. It started somewhere at the nape of her neck and shimmered down the length of her back.

For a second Leo's gaze just rested on her. She felt it like a tangible weight. Assessing her.

Then it was gone. Leo Makarios turned back and resumed his German conversation.

Mutely, Anna stayed at his side.

He kept her there for the rest of the evening.

It took all her professionalism to keep going. That and a dogged, grim determination that she was *not* going to let this get to her.

Let Leo Makarios get to her.

Because he was.

She could tell herself all she liked that to a man like Leo Makarios, surrounded as he was by chic, elegant, rich and aristocratic women from his own world, she was nothing but a walking jewellery display.

But why, then, was he keeping her at his side? And if her, then why not the other models in turn?

She said as much at one point. He had just disengaged himself gracefully from a Dutch banker and his wife, and had taken Anna's elbow to guide her towards the buffet tables.

'Isn't it time to show off the other stones now, Mr Makarios? There's Kate with the rubies—over there.'

She indicated where the brunette was gazing awestruck, or so it seemed to her, at one of the men in the group she was part of. He was, Anna recognised, the orchestra's conductor.

Leo Makarios's gaze flicked across to Kate.

'How could I deprive Antal Lukacs of his latest adoring fan?' he murmured sardonically. 'And such a young and beautiful one.'

Anna's eyes widened. 'That's Antal Lukacs?' Even she had heard of such a world-famous conductor.

The heavy-lidded eyes glanced down at her.

'Would you like to meet him?'

'I'm sure he's quite bored enough with people gushing all over him,' she said dismissively.

'Somehow,' Leo Makarios murmured, 'I can't see you *gushing* over anyone.' His voice became dryer suddenly, more critical. 'You are certainly quite unimpressed to be wearing jewels that every woman here envies you wearing.'

Anna looked up at him.

'They're just carbon crystals—valued only because they are rare. Lots of other common crystals are just as beautiful. Diamonds are only worth money—'

'They are the Levantsky diamonds! Works of art in their own right,' Leo said sharply.

She shrugged. 'So is Mozart's music—and that doesn't cost millions to enjoy!'

The dark eyes rested on her. She watched them narrow very slightly. She did not look away. Why should she?

'I was told,' he said softly—and it was that same softness that had raised the hair on the nape of her neck earlier '—that you have an attitude issue. Lose it.'

She smiled sweetly up at him. She could feel adrenaline start to run in her.

'Is that another of your instructions, Mr Makarios?'

For a long moment he looked at her. She felt the adrenaline curl around every cell in her body.

'What is your problem, Ms Delane?' he asked, in that same soft, deadly voice.

You, she wanted to say. *You're the problem.*

Then, even as she stared defiantly back at him, her false smile straightening to a thin, pressed line, something changed in his eyes.

He seemed to move minutely, as if closing her off from the rest of the room.

The lashes swept down over his eyes, and she felt the breath in her throat tighten.

'Don't fight me,' he said in a low voice. Then she could see it. Something else came into his eyes, something that made a hollow where her stomach usually was. 'You really are,' he added slowly, 'quite incredibly beautiful…'

Anna felt the hollow where her stomach had been turn slowly over.

No. She didn't want this happening. She didn't.

She opened her mouth to say so. Say something. Anything. But all she could do was stare. The room disappeared; the people disappeared; everything vanished. She was just standing, looking up at the man—letting him look at her. Look at her with those powerful heavy-lidded eyes, over which those long dark lashes were sweeping down.

The hollow where her stomach had been pooled with heat—

heat that was starting to spread out through the veins in her body, carried by her treacherous beating heart.

She saw him see it. See the way the heat was starting to flow through her body. The eyes, so dark, so lambent, narrowed. A smile curved along his wide, mobile mouth. It was a smile of acknowledgement, satisfaction.

Anticipation.

He murmured something to her. So quietly that in the buzz of noise and conversation all around Anna thought she must have imagined it.

Of course she had imagined it.

But for a moment she thought he had murmured, 'Later...'

Then, in an instant, his expression changed, becoming smooth and bland.

'Ah, Minister...'

The perambulation resumed. And Leo Makarios still kept Anna at his side.

Anna kicked off her shoes with a sense of relief. Then she peeled off the long black satin gloves, dropping them onto the dressing table stool in her room. Hooking her now bare fingers round her back, she started to undo the painstakingly fastened together dress. The diamonds had been handed back into the care of the security company, and finally the models had been free to go up to their rooms. Anna had hardly been able to wait.

God, the evening had been endless!

And more than that. Her nerves were shredded, stretched to breaking point.

Being touted around by Leo Makarios had been excruciating. She could feel the tension racking up in her.

He was getting to her, and she didn't like it. Not one bit.

Her lips pressed together. Spending time with the man the way she had should have *de*sensitised her to him. Should have made her get past that ridiculous disturbing rush she'd felt when he'd first walked in on the shoot and had such an impact on her. By now she should simply be able to see him abstractly, as a good-looking man. Exceptionally so, for a rich man—the combination was as rare as hen's teeth in her experience—but nothing more. Certainly not a man who should have the slightest effect on her.

Such as making her breath catch in her throat.

Heat flush through her.

Nerves quicken in awareness.

Electricity shoot through her.

No!

Grimly she stared at herself in the mirror over the dressing table.

Yes, she was slightly flushed; her eyes were a little wider than usual. But that was just because it had been a long day and a longer evening. She was tired, that was all.

She looked at her reflection defiantly.

Out of the glass stared back a familiar image. The black hair, the pale skin and the green eyes. Probably inherited from your dad—whoever he was—her gran had always told her. The dramatic, eye-catching features an accidental meshing of DNA that had just happened to produce a face that was beautiful.

But her beauty was just a commodity. She sold it, day after day, to anyone who paid the right price for it.

And that's all I sell.

Too many men thought otherwise. Thought she was also selling the right for them to look her up and down, strip her naked with their eyes, wonder what she was like in bed, offer to find out...

She turned away from the mirror sharply, continuing to undo, hook by hook, the simple but beautifully made dress.

At least she was free of the diamonds. The whole ridiculous glitter of them. Her eyes hardened again. Had Leo Makarios really not been able to see how overdone the whole lot was when worn together like that? That the sum was less than the individual pieces?

She shook her head in impatience. Who cared what Leo Makarios thought? About his wretched Levantsky diamonds or about her.

Or, she told herself doggedly, what she thought about him.

It's completely academic anyway. After this I'll never set eyes on him again. And then I'll be safe...

She stilled. Why had she used that word? She was safe from Leo Makarios right now! Yes, he'd cast his eye over her, and found her visually pleasing, but she'd obviously annoyed him with her attitude—and anyway, for heaven's sake, the man was in the middle of a glittering, glamorous party held to impress his rich pals—he wasn't going to take time out to chase around some clothes-horse he'd hired. And who said he wanted her in the first place? A man with his looks and money must have women queuing round the block for his attention. He could pick any woman he wanted from his glittering social circle. He was probably schmoozing some Austrian countess or Park Avenue princess right now.

So how come he clamped you to his side the whole evening?

She shrugged. Justin had probably warned him that her booker had called her 'difficult', and so Leo Makarios had just been keeping her in order—at his side.

A saying floated through her head.

Keep your friends close, but your enemies closer.

She frowned. Why had that come into her mind?

Leo Makarios was neither a friend nor an enemy.

He was a stranger. Nothing more.

And he was going to stay one.

That way, he'd never be dangerous to her.

CHAPTER THREE

LEO strolled down the long carpeted corridor, the two house-hold staff in front of him loaded down with trays.

He wasn't sure he'd ever been to this floor before. It wasn't the old servants' quarters in the attic, but nor was it guest apartments. But even if the rooms up here lacked the opulent extravagance of the main floors of the Schloss they were still very comfortably appointed. Just right for office staff or other employees. He wondered idly if the three models were all housed in a row. The redhead, of course, would be with Markos, in one of the lavish suites below. Would the blonde and the brunette have found somewhere else to sleep tonight? he mused. Maybe the brunette was busy adoring Antal Lukacs from close quarters, he though cynically, knowing the conductor's penchant for females. The blonde, though, had looked far too tense to be receptive to the admiration she had received during the evening.

None of them were of any interest to him, however. There was only one woman who had caught his eye, and she, he knew, had been highly receptive to him. Oh, she might have an attitude issue, but that was immaterial. It wouldn't last. He would see to that. He'd have her purring like a cat before long.

Women always purred for him.

The two staff stopped outside one of the doors and glanced back at him. He gave a nod, and one of them knocked discreetly.

Inside the room, Anna paused, dropping her hands from her back. What on earth…? The knock came again. Hastily doing up her hooks again, for decency's sake, she crossed over and opened the door. Outside were two of the household staff, each bearing a huge tray covered with a linen cloth.

'I'm sorry,' she said, taken aback. 'I mean—um—*Entschuldigen Sie bitte, aber Ich habe nicht...*'

Her sketchy German failed her. She had no idea how to say she had not ordered anything.

The man merely bowed slightly and swept in, followed by the second man. They set both trays down on the low table in front of a pair of armchairs by the window, and removed the cloths.

An entire light supper was contained on the trays—including, she saw, a bottle of chilled white wine, a flagon of orange juice, a jug of mineral water and a coffee pot.

'I'm afraid I didn't ask for—' she began.

'But I, however, did.' A deep, familiar voice interrupted her.

She whipped round. There, in the doorway, stood Leo Makarios.

For a moment Anna just stared, unable to believe her eyes.

Let alone what was happening.

He strolled into her room.

He was still in evening dress, still looking impeccable, as only a man of his height, wealth and looks could look, but there was a faint shadow along his jaw that somehow suddenly made him look—

Sexy.

The word came out of nowhere into her brain, and the moment it formed she was horrified.

She opened her mouth to say something. Anything. But her mind was a maelstrom of conflicting emotions. Predominant was disbelief. Sheer disbelief that Leo Makarios was strolling into her bedroom, one hand in his trouser pocket, looking as though he had every right to be there.

The two members of his household staff evidently thought so. They were diligently laying out their wares on the low table, deftly and neatly, placing a large plate of thinly sliced smoked chicken, ham and salmon together with a bowl of salad and a basket of bread in the centre, with porcelain plates and silver cutlery nestling in white damask napkins. Crystal glasses followed suit, and then a coffee service and drinks and a plate of tiny chocolate truffles.

'Won't you sit down?' said Leo Makarios, indicating one of the armchairs. He simultaneously lowered his tall frame into the other one.

What the hell do you think you're doing? She wanted to scream at him.

But the presence of the two staff made it impossible. Good grief, the last thing she wanted was to make a public scene that would inevitably feed back into the gossip machine that was always at work around the rich and famous.

Every nerve screwed tight, she urged them mentally to clear out. Because the moment they were gone she would—

'Gnadige Fraulein?' One of the staff was indicating her chair, bowing politely. The other was busy opening the wine.

Oh, hell, she would have to sit down, pretend that—my goodness—no, of course there was nothing strange in the castle's multimillionaire owner turning up to have a little midnight supper with her!

Stiffly, she sat down, carefully ensuring the narrow skirts of her excruciatingly valuable dress were not catching on anything. Her face was a mask. But behind the mask her emotions were tumbling like a wash cycle set to crazy.

Skirts settled, and ignoring the fact that her back was imperfectly fastened, she looked up, ready to aim a killing glare at him.

Instead, she just stared, the breath stalling in her throat.

Leo Makarios was loosening his dress tie and slipping the top button on his shirt.

That, and the shadowed jawline, made her heart stop beating.

Oh, dear God, he is just so—

The word slipped straight into her mind—right out of her subconscious.

Sexy.

It was that word again, coming out of nowhere—refusing to go. She had heard it a million times—it was one of the most popular in the fashion world. But it had never meant anything at all to her. It was just people posing and pouting and putting it on for the camera or an audience.

With Leo Makarios it was real.

And it was, she realised, standing there as if someone had punched her in the solar plexus, incredibly powerful.

She tried desperately to analyse it away. It was just the juxtaposition of contrasting modes, that was all—the severe formality of the tuxedo with the raffish informality of a loosened tie and shirt, accentuated by the roughened jawline.

But the effect didn't diminish. Quite the reverse, it simply gained potency, aided and abetted by the way his lean frame lounged back in supreme ease, long legs stretched out, hands curved over the arms of the chair, head resting on the chairback, those dark heavy-lidded eyes resting on her.

Looking at her.

Letting her look back.

Suddenly she did not want the household staff to disappear. She didn't want to be alone with Leo Makarios.

Anna could feel a heat flaring out from somewhere deep inside her. She tried to douse it, extinguish it, but it wouldn't be cooled. Instead it curled and spread through her as she just sat there, drinking in the man sitting opposite her, now being offered a taste of the wine that had just been opened.

She saw him sample the wine, saw him nod, saw the member of staff turn to fill her glass and then his employer's, then be dismissed with his colleague, saw them both bowing briefly and then quitting the room, shutting the door behind them.

Leaving her alone with Leo Makarios.

With huge effort she quashed down the dangerous pooling heat inside her.

She opened her mouth to speak, protest his uninvited presence.

But Leo Makarios was before her.

'Well,' he said, *'Mahlzeit.'*

Anna's mouth snapped shut again.

'What?'

'Mahlzeit,' he repeated, in his accented voice. His eyes

gleamed slightly. 'Have you not heard that yet? Austrians invariably pronounce that to each other before eating. It means mealtime. It appears to be their version of *bon appetit*. Now, what may I help you to?'

He picked up the serving spoon and fork and let them hover over the plate of meats and salmon.

She took a deep breath.

'Mr Makarios—' she began.

He looked up. 'Leo,' he said. 'I think we can dispense with the formalities now. *Theos*, it's been a long evening! But,' he went on, calmly selecting a slice of smoked chicken and placing it on her empty plate, 'a highly successful one. Ham and salmon?'

'No, thank you,' she snapped. 'Mr Makarios, I—'

The dark eyes lifted to her.

'Leo,' he said softly. 'So, just chicken, then?' He placed another slice on her plate. 'Salad?'

'No! I don't want any food. I don't want—'

He scooped up some salad and added it to her plate.

'I ate very little this evening, and you ate absolutely nothing. You must be hungry.'

I'm always hungry, she wanted to snap. But if I eat I'll put on weight and lose jobs. So I don't eat. And I ignore hunger!

But even as the words formed in her mind she felt a treacherous pang in her stomach. She didn't usually starve herself as she had done this evening. That was just counter-productive. But tonight had been so nerve-racking because of having to stay glued to Leo's side that the very idea of eating some of the buffet food, however delicious, had been impossible. She had planned to have herbal tea and an orange—she never travelled without either—to see her through to breakfast in the morning.

But the sight and smell of the beautifully prepared and presented food was so enticing. The hunger pang came again. The scent of a freshly baked roll wafted to her. She felt her will-power weaken.

All right—she would eat a light supper, a very light supper, and then throw Leo Makarios out. It was perfectly obvious what he'd turned up here for—

Or was it?

Had she got it completely wrong?

He had started to speak again.

'Tell me,' he said, as he helped himself to food, 'have you known the other three models long?'

Anna paused in the middle of lifting her fork to start eating. Chicken and salad without dressing wouldn't be a crime—and she would, of course, ignore the rolls.

'I beg your pardon?' Her voice sounded surprised at his question.

He repeated it, shaking out a white damask napkin on his lap and lifting his plate.

She took a mouthful of chicken, which melted in her mouth. 'I've known Jenny for several years, but this is the first time I've worked with Kate and Vanessa.'

'Which one is the redhead?' Leo Makarios asked.

'That would be Vanessa,' Anna replied with exaggerated politeness. 'The one with the big boobs, in case you need another way of identifying her.' Her voice was acid.

Dark eyes flicked over her.

'You really do need to lose that attitude,' Leo Makarios murmured.

'So do you,' she bit back. 'Models do have names, as well as bodies.'

She forked up a large amount of salad with unnecessary vigour.

'You take offence where none is intended—I merely had not yet managed to distinguish the four of you by name, only hair colour,' he replied coolly. The eyes rested on her momentarily. She thought she saw irritation in them.

Was that supposed to be a reprimand? Anna wondered. If so, no sale.

She gave an indifferent shrug. 'Why do you ask about Vanessa?' she prompted. She was both relieved that he was not here for the reason she had assumed and warily curious as to why he was asking about his cousin's girlfriend. Maybe, she thought suddenly, Leo Makarios was in poaching mode. Not, however, that Vanessa had eyes for anyone other than this guy's cousin. Talk about stars in her eyes…the girl had it bad. Anna only hoped she wouldn't get hurt—but she wasn't taking bets on it.

He took a mouthful of wine.

'If you do not know her well, my enquiry will mean little,' he answered.

'Yes, well, what little I do know of her is that she's a nice girl.' Anna replied all the same—pointedly. 'Nice, if dumb,' she added.

Leo Makarios's eyebrows pulled together, making him look forbidding somehow.

'Dumb?' There was a bite in his voice she'd have been deaf not to hear.

'Dumb enough to fall for your cousin, I mean,' she elucidated.

The forbidding look suddenly became even more intense.

Anna gave him an old-fashioned look. 'Oh, come on—your fancy cousin hardly looks like a down-on-one-knee kind of guy! Vanessa's going to get burned—big-time. It's totally obvious.'

'My cousin is very generous to his mistresses,' Leo Makarios informed her. There was hauteur in his face now, and a repressive note in his voice.

A choking sound escaped Anna.

'Mistresses? Last time I looked, crinolines were definitely out of fashion!'

He frowned again.

'I do not understand your reference.'

'It means mistresses went out with Queen Victoria. Mistresses—kept women—rich protectors, you know.'

A cynical curve indented his mouth.

'You think women no longer like to take rich men as their lovers, and thereby live in a style that they could not afford for themselves?'

Her eyes hardened. He was right, damn it—her exposure to the realities of life in the fashion world had taught her that a long time ago.

'If they do, then 'mistress' is not the term I'd use for them,' she riposted.

'What would you use then?'

'One unfit for mixed company.' She gave her acid-sweet smile again. 'And, by the way, no—I do *not* count Vanessa as one of them!'

'You are so sure of that?' The cynical note was back in his voice.

Anna glared at him.

'Yes,' she said. 'I am. I just hope she's got a best friend to mop her up when your cousin gets bored with being adored and moves on to his next squeeze.'

The dark eyebrows drew together again.

'I have already told you that Markos has no reason not to be generous to her when he ends their affair.'

Anna gave up. There was clearly no point discussing the matter. Vanessa was going to get hurt, and if good old Markos was anything like his lovely cousin then it was going to be tears after bedtime for sure.

'You can't dry your eyes on diamonds,' she contented herself with answering dryly.

'She is a very beautiful woman—she will soon find another lover.'

The indifference in his voice raised her hackles.

'Oh, good—that's all right, then.' Anna bestowed another acid smile on him.

But Leo Makarios was frowning again—and then a different expression was on his face.

'What you say is disturbing,' he said slowly. 'You believe she has ambitions for marriage?'

'Ambitions?' Anna sat back. Her chicken and salad were gone, and she wasn't about to help herself to any more. The pangs had been stilled, and it was time to get rid of Mr Money-Bags Makarios—and his delightful views on female venality.

'I'd say she probably has some fairy-tale vision of wafting down an aisle to a heavenly choir towards your cousin suddenly transformed into Prince Charming with a halo, but she can't possibly be idiotic enough to think a man like your cousin is going to *marry* her!'

Leo Makarios's mouth tightened.

'Perhaps you could ensure,' he said, resting his eyes on her, 'that she understands that that is indeed the case. She must harbour no ambitions to entrap Markos into marriage.'

Anna reached for the water. 'I'll be sure to pass the message on,' she said dryly.

'A naïve woman can be even more dangerous than a clever one,' he rejoined darkly.

Dangerous. Suddenly Anna wished he hadn't used that particular word. It was the one that had been haunting her about *him* ever since she'd set eyes on him.

Of their own volition her eyes swept across to him.

He seemed to be lost in thought, heavy-lidded eyes inward-looking, a brooding expression on his face. Preoccupied as he was, she could not resist indulging in just gazing at him a moment.

Oh, dear God, he really was gorgeous! She just stared at him, as if he were a forbidden cream cake in a baker's shop. Then, forcing herself, she dragged her eyes away and finished pouring out her glass of water. She drank it down and set the glass back on the table.

She gave herself a mental shake. Whatever her first assumptions had been about why Leo Makarios had swanned in here at this time of night, it was clear she'd been completely wrong. He was simply here on an intelligence-gathering mission—the purpose of which was to protect his precious cousin from women who—shock, horror—fell in love with him.

Leo wasn't here to pounce. In fact he was probably just using up some rare spare time while a piece of posh totty slipped into her couture negligee and buffed her nails in his state apartment downstairs. Rich men, she knew, from her years in the fashion world, did odd things at odd times. Being eccentric, like turning up complete with a midnight supper just to get the gen on his cousin's squeeze, was one of the perks of being so loaded you could do what you liked and no one even blinked.

She watched him polish off the last of his meal. He definitely had a large frame to fill up. Not that there was the slightest sign of fat on him. All lean muscle. A lot of power and vigour at his disposal. Whoever was waiting for him was clearly in for an energetic night...

No—stop that! Her self-admonishment was instant and severe. The less she thought about Leo Makarios's sex life—which had *nothing* to do with her!—the better. In fact, the sooner he was out of here the better. The hooks at the back of her dress were digging into her, and she was dying to get her make-up off and have a shower.

Well, he wouldn't be long now, surely?

Leo set his plate down, picked up his wine glass, and leant back again.

'You are not drinking your wine,' he remarked.

'Empty calories,' she answered flippantly.

The frown came again.

'Why do you starve yourself?'

Anna shrugged. 'Some models have fast metabolisms and can eat a horse and not show it. Jenny's like that. Me, I'll just pile on the pounds if I eat.' She gave a twisted smile. 'I'll eat when I retire,' she said.

Why was she talking to him? She wanted him to finish his wine and go.

'Retire? But you are how old?'

She made a face. 'Long in the tooth for modelling. The cult is for youth—the younger the better.'

'Ridiculous! Who would want the bud instead of the full flower?'

'Modelling agencies,' she said succinctly. 'Young girls are a lot more malleable—controllable and exploitable. It's a nasty business, modelling.'

'And yet...' his eyes rested on her '...you thrive.'

'I survive,' she corrected him. 'But,' she went on, 'I'm not ungrateful. Modelling's been a well-paid career for me.'

There was a shuttered look on his face suddenly.

'Money is important to you?'

Anna looked at him. 'I'd be pretty stupid if it weren't! I've known models blowing the whole damn lot they earn—chucking it around on clothes and rich living—and they end up with nothing to show for it.'

'But you are more shrewd?' The heavy-lidded eyes were resting on her.

'I hope so.' She returned his look, keeping it level. His expression stayed shuttered.

Then suddenly, out of nowhere, it changed.

And Anna's breath stopped.

He was looking at her. Just looking at her.

How can a look stop me breathing? Breathe—for God's sake, breathe!

But she couldn't. The breathlessness was absolute, endless.

And as she just sat there, the breath frozen in her lungs, her stomach seemed to be doing a very long, slow motion flip inside her.

Anna felt her hands close over the arms of her chair. Felt, as if from a long, long distance away, her muscles tense as she levered herself to her feet. But, like a mirror image, Leo Makarios was doing the same—getting to his feet.

He was coming towards her.

It was obvious why. Totally, absolutely obvious. And it had been from the moment the expression in his eyes had changed.

Changed to one of intent.

An intent that should have been making her body react the way it always did when she saw that kind of look in a man's eyes.

But no man had ever looked like that at her before. With lust, yes; with speculation; with hot, hungry appetite; with eagerness and with expectation.

Never the way Leo Makarios was looking at her.

Anna's legs felt weak; her heart was hammering. A voice

seemed to be inside her head, shouting *Danger!* As if it was some kind of automated warning.

A warning she could do absolutely nothing about—was helpless to heed.

He was coming towards her.

Tall, so tall. Lean, with a clear purposefulness about him. The dark eyes never left her, the expression in them turning her insides to water.

She still couldn't breathe, couldn't move. Just stood there, like a statue, immobile, lips parted, gazing at the planes of his face, his wide, mobile mouth, the loosened tie, the open-necked shirt, with waves of weakness going through her.

Leo stopped. Reached out a hand for her. With a slow, controlled movement he drew a single forefinger down her cheek.

It melted her skin where it touched.

And went on melting.

'You really are,' he said, 'exquisitely lovely.'

The eyes changed again, becoming lambent.

'Exquisite,' he echoed softly.

And all Anna could do was just stand there, transfixed, as those heavy-lidded eyes rested on her, draining from her all will, all resistance.

Because in their lambent depths was something she had never seen before.

It was desire.

Not lust. Not slime. Not appetite.

Just—*desire*.

Desire—burning with a clear, ineluctable, irresistible flame...

Again that wave of weakness drowned through her, draining from her everything she had ever felt before about men looking at her...

Because nothing, *nothing* she had ever felt before, was anything like this.

She waited for the anger, the biting, aggressive anger that always came when some man looked at her with only one purpose, one intent in his mind.

But it didn't come.

Instead, a slow-dissolving honey seemed to be spreading out through her veins, warming and weakening her, making her almost sway with sudden debilitating bonelessness.

His eyes were half closed, it seemed, their heavy lids lowered in a sweep of long black lashes. Her breath caught again, another spoon of honey spilling slowly through her veins.

She felt her lips part. As if she did not even have the strength to hold her mouth closed. She felt her eyelids flicker heavily, her pupils dilate.

Her body swayed. Very, very slightly.

He was so close to her. So close. She could feel his presence in her body space, catch the scent of his musk mingled with the expensive notes of his aftershave, heady and spiced. She could see the roughened jawline, the wide, mobile mouth, the lean, tanned cheek—and those heavy, half-closed eyes with the clear, clear intent in them.

Slowly, her insides turned over again.

'Exquisite,' he murmured again.

One hand slid around her neck, the other to her waist, and he lowered his mouth to hers, tongue sliding effortlessly within the silken confines.

For a timeless, delicious moment Leo luxuriated in the feel of her mouth. Silky, sensual, and so very, very arousing.

Not that he needed to be aroused. True, he had taken the opportunity while he was eating to sound her out about the redhead who seemed to have captivated his cousin—in respect of which prudence alone dictated that he warn his cousin off the girl. Markos was no gullible fool—far from it—but still, who knew how stupid a man could be if he was subjected to enough adoring gazes like those Leo had been witnessing all evening? Maybe they were calculated and maybe not. But if they weren't—and they had, he acknowledged, looked genuine—then Markos might be at greater risk than he knew. At the very least the girl would be difficult to dislodge, and would probably cause a tearful scene when the inevitable end came, which he wouldn't wish on any man. At the worst—well, although tears and weeping wouldn't wash with himself—Markos might just be more vulnerable, and find himself in deeper water than he was comfortable with. A naïve woman, entertaining fantasies about marriage, Leo realised, could be far more dangerous than one who knew which way the world went round.

Like the woman he was enjoying now.

Anna was exactly what he wanted. There'd been a lot of tension surrounding the launch of the Levantsky marque, and he'd put a lot of personal effort into ensuring that tonight and tomorrow were being organised the way he wanted them to be. That, of course, was on top of his normal non-stop business schedule. It might annoy him, but it didn't surprise him, that something had had to give—and that something was his sex life. It had been nearly a month since he had parted company with the Italian divorcee with whom he had been more than happy to celebrate her new sexual freedom, and there had been no time to choose her successor.

So the sable-haired beauty in his arms had caught his attention at a timely moment. She was just what he needed. A sophisticated, independent, unattached woman who had made it more than clear that she was receptive to his attentions. The world she moved in was known for its liberal sexual habits, and she doubtless had her pick of lovers in her time. Her caustic tongue and attitude might well put some men off, but it didn't bother him. It could just be put on for effect, anyway, to make herself stand out from the competition—deliberately assumed to catch the attention of men like him, jaded by fawning women.

Whatever the cause, it certainly wasn't in evidence now. She was reacting just the way he'd known she would—letting him taste her to the full and taking her own pleasure in it.

Leisurely, Leo slid his hand over her hip. Though slender, it was not in the least bony—for which he was glad. There was a rounded softness there beneath the silk of her dress that was really very enticing.

He deepened the kiss, pulling her body closer against his. He could feel his own body reacting very pleasurably to the contact. Rich anticipation filled him. A month's celibacy might have been unwelcome, but it had its compensations.

Tonight would be good, he knew.

She would be good.

Letting his tongue powerfully stroke hers, he felt her yield to him, and he liked that. Too many women these days started a competition when he was kissing them, presumably thinking he found it exciting. They did not appreciate—as this one did—just how very erotic it was for a man to feel a woman being pleasured by him…

He felt his arousal strengthen. A month's starvation had made him hungry.

Hungry for much more than a mere appetiser. Time to take their table for the main course.

He drew his mouth back a little, just enough to allow him to softly bite her swollen lower lip.

'Shall we?' he said, his mouth curving sensually, his lashes sweeping down over his eyes. He exerted the slightest pressure at her hip, loosening his hand from her neck to guide her towards the bed.

As he released her she swayed slightly, eyes dazed. A small frown started to form between his eyes.

Was she drunk? She'd nursed a single glass of champagne all evening, and it had still been almost as full at the end as at the beginning. And just now, over supper, she had stuck entirely to water. So why was she swaying? Looking dazed and dizzy?

Or was it merely sexual arousal? Her pupils were wide and dilated, lips swollen, parted. His eyes flickered downward, and then his mouth curved into a relaxing smile. Her breasts were straining against the confines of her dress, and even without the help of the laced corset, the soft mounds were swelling deliciously above her bodice.

He felt his own arousal surge through his body. Of its own volition his hand reached, curved around one lovely, tempting orb, thumb brushing the dark silk where the nipple strained against it.

He wanted her, badly. Now.

'You really are...' his voice was husky '...so very tempting.' His thumb brushed again, and he felt himself thicken at the contact. Unable to resist, he started to close in on her. He wanted that mouth once more, that silken lushness...

The crack of her palm against his cheek took him totally and completely by surprise.

Anna hauled herself back. Her heart was hammering in her chest, pounding as if she'd done a workout. Panic, horror and a whole storm of emotions she couldn't even identify poured through her like a deluge.

'What the *hell*—?'

Leo Makarios was staring at her, shock naked on his face. Where her hand had impacted was a red mark.

Anna jerked further back.

'Get out of here. Just get out!'

He was standing stock still. Every line of his body taut.

'You will tell me,' he bit out, '*exactly* what that was for!'

Her eyes flashed. Her breathing was ragged, tumultuous, her heart still pounding. Adrenaline was surging through her—and a whole lot more.

'How dare you? How dare you think you can help yourself to me? Get *out*!'

His face darkened, his eyes suddenly as hard as steel.

'It's a little late,' he spelt out, his voice harsh, contemptuous, 'to tell me that.' His eyes narrowed. 'I don't like teases. Don't say yes to me and then change your mind and blame me for it.'

Anna's eyes distended.

'Say yes? I never said yes!'

'You've been saying yes all evening,' he bit back. 'From the moment I first set eyes on you. You made it crystal-clear you wanted me. Right up to ten seconds ago. Don't pretend to be naïve.' The voice was still harsh, still contemptuous. Two lines of white were etched around his mouth, colour flaring along his cheekbones.

She took a thin, hissing breath, eyes aflame with fury.

'My God, you have a nerve. I don't have to take this from you. Go and find some other willing floozy for the night! How dare you think you can use me for a night's entertainment?'

'Forgive me, but you gave every impression that *you* were willing.' The sneer in his voice was open.

Anna's eyes spat fire. Oh, how she wanted to feel anger! She was feeling it now all right. Coruscating, burning, biting, furious, incandescent anger. She was shaking with it.

'Get *out*! I don't have to take this! I don't have to put up with men who think because I model clothes I'll take them off for them whenever they feel like it. Now get out of my room before I charge you for harassment!'

Leo's face was as if carved from marble.

'Be very careful,' he told her, his eyes like chips of rock, 'what you say to me.'

Her face contorted.

'Don't threaten me. I don't have to be treated like this by you or anyone else—however stinking rich they are!'

'Don't tell me—' the contemptuous note was back in his voice '—it's in your contract.'

'Well, it's just as bloody well it is, isn't it?' she spat back at him. 'Because with you around I need it!'

The eyes were like granite again.

'Enough. You have made your point of view very clear. But next time you want to play the outraged virtue card, Ms Delane, I suggest you do it *before* you entertain a man in your bedroom at midnight.'

He threw a last stony, contemptuously angry look at her, and walked out.

The door shut behind him with a violent reverberating thud.

Leo strode down the corridor in a cold rage such as he had seldom experienced.

Christos, where the hell had that come from?

From temptress to virago in ten seconds flat!

Deliberate?

His eyes narrowed. If there'd been the slightest indication that the whole thing was a put-on he'd—

He felt his hands clench as he walked rapidly away, and he had to force himself to release them.

No, she wasn't worth it. Whether or not she was putting it on—one of those women who enjoyed blowing hot then cold just to twist men up—he didn't care. Let her enjoy her virtue. *Theos*, it was all she was going to enjoy tonight.

Anna Delane could enjoy her precious celibacy, and he…he could have a cold shower.

How the hell was I supposed to know she didn't want it?

Indignation filled him—and a sense of unjustified ill usage.

Good God, he wasn't some callow teenager, unable to tell whether a woman was responding to him. Anna Delane had responded all right—clear and loud.

So why the outrage?

Roughly, he pushed the question aside. What the hell did he care what the answer was?

His interest in Anna Delane was over.

Permanently.

CHAPTER FOUR

ANNA lay in bed. Her heart was still pumping, adrenaline surging through her. She couldn't stop it. Her whole body was as tense as a board, every muscle rigid.

How had it come to this? How?

Disbelief kept flooding through her, cold and icy through her guts.

The cold emptied through her again, clutching at her with its icy fingers.

How, *how* had it happened?

The question went round and round, pounding ceaselessly, tormentingly.

How had she let Leo Makarios do that to her? Just walk up to her and start to touch her. And she'd done nothing—*nothing*! Pathetic. *Pathetic.*

A shudder went through her.

She had just let him stand there and kiss her, *fondle* her, as if she was some kind of...some kind of...

She felt anger excoriating her. Anger at Leo Makarios, who had just walked into her bedroom and decided to help himself to her. The anger wired through her nerves. Anger at Leo Makarios.

But a worse fury consumed her too.

Anger at herself.

How could she have succumbed to him like that? Letting him come into her room, kiss her, caress her, do what he wanted to her? How could he have just swept away all her defences, all her years of fighting men off?

And into her head stole a voice that chilled her to the bone.

Because you didn't want to fight him off. You wanted him...you wanted him badly...Wanted to feel his mouth on yours, wanted his hands caressing you, wanted to feel him stroke you, arouse you...

She closed her eyes in anguish, her face contorting.

No, please—please. She mustn't want Leo Makarios.

Not a man like that, a man who's just proved himself to be everything you knew he was. Everything! The kind of man who wants instant cheap gratification and thinks you're going to roll over and let him get it from you!

Revulsion shuddered through her.

Then slowly, agonisingly slowly, piece by piece, she started to pull herself together.

Yes, she had been a fool, an idiot, but the worst had not happened—that was what she must hang on to. It might have been so close to the edge of the precipice that she must never, ever think of it again, but at least she had summoned the last of her sanity and sent him packing.

She opened her eyes again, staring into the dark.

Imagine if it were now after you'd given yourself totally to him. If you were lying here now and he'd gone back to his gilded state apartment, sleek and sated, leaving you here with nothing left but the bones...

Cold iced through her again.

She had had such a narrow escape...

But she *had* escaped—that was what she must remember. She had clawed back to sanity just in time.

And she was safe now. Safe.

Slowly, very slowly, she felt her heart-rate come down.

Never, ever again would Leo Makarios push her that close to the precipice.

Never.

Her mouth thinned.

Never.

'Plunge your hands in. Now lift them out—lift, lift, lift! Yes. Hold them up! Up!'

Anna held her hands the way she was being told to. So did the other three models. They were standing around the vast oak table in the castle's echoing hall again, but this time none of them was wearing any of the Levantsky jewels.

Their hands were all in a huge golden bowl into which had been poured rivers of diamonds, emeralds, rubies and sapphires. And now the four models were plunging into this golden cornucopia and lifting them out, their fingers dripping necklaces and earrings and bracelets.

'*Basta!*' Tonio Embrutti called, simultaneously summoning the stylist and her assistants. 'Now I want the jewels just draped over their shoulders, in their hair, over their arms, their breasts. Not fastened, just draped.'

His pudgy face took on a sulky look. 'Of course, their bodies *should* be naked, but—'

He contented himself with merely making an Italian gesture of exasperation with his hands, waving his camera around as he did so.

Anna stood patiently as the stylist's assistants got to work.

Her mind was strangely numb. She'd got hardly any sleep last night, and the disapproving make-up artist had commented adversely on the effect thereof on her eyes and complexion. Anna didn't care. She was, she knew, beyond caring. She had only one overriding impulse.

To get out of here. Out and home.

But she still had today and tonight to get through before she could run. At least today there was no sign of Leo Makarios. He'd gone off with his guests—some whisked off to ski slopes, some on horse-drawn sleigh rides, some on helicopter tours of the Austrian Alps, or back to Vienna and Munich for shopping trips.

Even so, today's shoot seemed longer than yesterday's, but finally it was done. Released at last, changed back into her normal clothes, Anna headed back up to her room. Vanessa had disappeared instantly—presumably Markos was in the wings somewhere—and Kate almost as quickly.

'There's an early concert in the town's Musikverein,' Kate had explained to the others eagerly. 'Maestro Lukacs has given me a ticket!' She'd said it as though he'd given her the keys to the kingdom, her eyes shining.

'Have fun,' Anna had said dryly. Preferably, she added silently, not in Antal Lukacs's bed. Kate was far too impressionable.

She headed off after Jenny, also making for her room. The other model had a head start on her up the vast stairs. Anna sprinted after her.

'Wait for me!' she called. But Jenny was ploughing on, reaching the set of stairs that led to the upper floors. She seemed to be walking faster and faster, as if the devil was driving her.

But then it was, Anna knew. Her face shadowed. God, she might have been an idiot the night before, letting Leo Makarios get to within a hair's breadth of tumbling her down into bed, but at least she'd found her sanity in time! Jenny had never found hers with the man who had got her into this mess. And now she was facing the complete disintegration of her life. Forced to cash in everything she had and flee.

Flee to keep her baby safe from the man who would take it from her.

Anna's eyes darkened. Well, whatever it took she would make sure she stood by Jenny! Money, support—someone there at the birth of her child—whatever Jenny needed, she'd stick by her.

But right now Jenny just needed reassurance. Someone to keep her spirits up, take away the edge of fear that was eating into her day by day at the thought of her pregnancy being discovered.

Anna hurried on, up the second flight of stairs and along the corridor to her bedroom. Jenny had rushed ahead and was out of sight. Anna paused outside her friend's door, wondering whether Jenny would like a cup of tea with her.

'Jen, do you want a cuppa? Rosehip or chamomile?'

There was no answer.

Anna opened the door and poked her head round. Maybe Jenny was in the bathroom.

She wasn't.

She was sitting on her bed. Like Anna, she was wearing trousers, but unlike Anna she had a large, fleecy long-sleeved pullover on.

And out of the sleeve she was sliding a long ruby bracelet.

For one long, timeless moment Anna did not believe what she was seeing. And then, with a rush of icy water in her stomach, she stepped into the room, closing the door behind her.

Jenny was staring at her. Staring at her with shock and fear naked on her face. She was as white as a sheet, every bone in her face starkly outlined.

Slowly, Anna came forward.

'Oh, my God, Jen, what have you done?'

Her voice was hollow.

Jenny just stared; she was beyond speech, Anna could see— wound up so tight she would break if stressed any further.

Carefully, Anna went and sat down beside her.

Jenny turned huge distended eyes on her.

'Do you know—' her voice sounded taut and strange '—Khalil wanted to give me a ruby bracelet? I said no. He wanted to give me lots of jewels, but I always said no. It made him angry, I know. He hid it, but it did.' Her eyes went down to the ruby bracelet lying across the palm of her hand, winking in the lamplight.

'It's ironic, isn't it?' she said, and her voice still had that strange breaking quality about it. 'If I'd just taken one, just one of all the jewels he wanted to give me, I'd be all right now. I could sell it and have enough...enough money to...to escape with. But I never took them. Not one. Even though he wanted to give them to me.'

She touched one of the stones with her finger.

Carefully, very carefully, Anna spoke.

'But these aren't Khalil's jewels, Jen. And he never gave them to you.' She paused. 'I'll take the bracelet back.'

She reached across to lift it from Jenny's palm. For a moment so brief it hardly happened she saw Jenny's fingers start to claw shut over the bracelet. Then, as if exerting a vast invisible effort, the fingers stilled.

'You can't keep it, Jen. You know you can't.'

Anna's voice was quiet, reassuring.

Slowly Jenny opened her palm completely, letting the glittering stones run red across her hand. She stared down at them.

Anna lifted them away. Her heart was beating fast, the icy water still in her stomach. Slowly she got to her feet. Her mind was racing, almost going into panic. But she mustn't panic—she mustn't.

What the hell am I going to do?

And, shooting right through her panicking brain, came one grim question.

How long have we got before it's discovered missing?

Claws pincered in her stomach. The security arrangements for the Levantsky jewels were draconian. They had to be, obviously. Every time they were brought out or put away—either for a shoot, or for her and the other models to wear the night before—security guards were all over the place. Every item was catalogued and signed in and out on a computerised check system personally entered by Leo Makarios's sidekick, Justin.

So how the hell had Jenny walked off with a bracelet?

There was no time to think about that—no time to do anything except hope and pray she could somehow, anyhow, get the bracelet back.

Back where, though?

She could hardly just swan up to Justin and calmly inform him he'd missed a piece! Everyone would go totally ballistic! There'd be a full-scale Spanish Inquisition, and that would end up with every damn finger in the Schloss pointing at Jenny!

And that was all Jenny needed! Police sirens and lawyers and the press—and a prison sentence for theft.

Because one thing was for sure. Leo Makarios was not the type to let anyone, *anyone* waltz off with a single Levantsky jewel!

She swallowed. She must not panic Jenny. Whatever happened, that was essential. Jenny was on the edge of a total breakdown, she could see. Well, already over the edge, actually, she realised, if she'd been driven to try and walk off with a priceless ruby bracelet...

Anna forced her voice to sound calm.

'Don't go anywhere, Jen. Just stay here. And don't answer the door unless it's me. Promise?'

The other girl still seemed to be in a state of shock. Anna wasn't surprised. God knew what state she must have been in to even think of taking any of the Levantsky jewels—and as for actually taking any...

Her stomach churning, panic nipping at her, Anna slipped out of Jenny's bedroom, hastily stuffing the bracelet inside the pocket of her trousers.

Its weight hung like a dead, accusing albatross.

She felt sick with fear.

Leo could hear his mobile vibrating deep beneath his skiing jacket as he slewed to a halt at the end of the run. With the light gone, his guests were discarding their skis and getting ready to board the waiting fleet of four-by-fours to take them back down to the Schloss.

Leo wished each and every one of them to perdition. He'd had to smile and converse and be a good host all damn day, and totally hide from them that inside he was in a worse mood than he could recall for a very long time. His temper was evil. He could feel it, lashing around inside him, not allowed an outlet.

But he knew exactly what outlet it wanted.

And it was one it wasn't going to get.

He wanted that damn girl, and he wasn't going to have her.

Anna Delane.

Sable-haired and breathtakingly desirable...

All through a night in which sleep had been persistently and exasperatingly scarce, all through a day which had tested his patience to the limit with its demanding and tedious social requirements, her image had kept intruding. He had banished it a hundred times, and it still came back.

And more than an image.

His memory was tactile.

Erotically, sensually tactile.

The feel of her silken mouth beneath his, the swelling roundness of her breast in his hand, the straining peak rigid beneath his stroking thumb, his body hardening against hers...

With savage control he hammered down the pointless, treacherous thoughts that heated through him.

OK, so he was frustrated. That was all. He'd gone a month without sex, and for him that was a long time. Last night had been punishing because he'd been on the brink of sexual release and then he'd been balked of it. No wonder his body was protesting!

But it was more than his body, he knew. If, say, he'd been interrupted by some kind of business emergency he'd have been a lot less angry than he was now. It wasn't just the absence of sex that was winding him up tighter than a watch spring.

It was her—that black-haired, green-eyed witch, who'd given him every damn come-on in the book and then called time on him in an outburst of self-righteous outrage as if he were one down from some kind of lascivious groper!

Thee mou, but she had wanted it as much as he had. She'd been melting for him, soft and honeyed, aroused and responsive.

And then to turn on him like that. Make those accusations, those spitting, contemptible accusations of harassment, *harassment*—

He felt his anger bite viciously.

A *liar*—that was what she was. Saying no when her body said yes. Had been saying yes all evening to him. All the way until he'd been about to lower her down on her bed...

With monumental effort he slammed shut the lid on his snarling thoughts. He would simply put Anna Delane out of his head, and that was that. There were plenty of other women around—*willing* women—who didn't play infantile and hypocritical games about sex.

Plenty who would be *happy* to be taken up as his mistress!

The trouble was, he couldn't think of any right now who held the slightest interest for him.

Damn Anna Delane. Turning him on—and then turfing him out! Well, she'd made her decision and so had he. He would *not* waste any more of his valuable time thinking about her.

With a rasp of irritation he realised his mobile had started to vibrate again. Hell, was he to have no peace at all? Impatiently he jabbed his ski-sticks into the snow and yanked out his phone.

'Yes?' he demanded icily, wanting only to dispose of the call and detach his skis.

But when he heard Justin's strained, panic-stricken voice, his body stilled completely.

Anna kept walking along the corridor. Her hands felt clammy, her heartbeat erratic, every muscle tense.

What am I going to do?

She still hadn't the faintest idea how she was to return the bracelet. She had to do something with it—anything—anything other than keep it on her person or in any way let its loss be linked back to Jenny.

She must have been mad to take it—

No! No time to think about that now! She'd cope with Jenny's breakdown later—her only priority now was to get rid of the bracelet.

She could just dump it somewhere. Somewhere it would be easily found by one of the household staff or something.

For a moment she thought of trying to tell someone that it had been taken completely by mistake, that its catch had got caught up in some material or something. But even as she ran it through her brain she knew it wouldn't wash. They hadn't been wearing their own clothes when the jewellery had been collected back in. They'd still been in their fashion shoot dresses. If any jewels had got caught they'd have been caught in them, not in the girls' mufti clothes.

How had she managed to take it?

Out of the blue, Anna suddenly knew. There'd been a shot with the four of them gathered around the table, their four pairs of hands buried wrist-deep in the golden bowl of priceless Levantsky jewels, spotlights blazing down at them to bring out every last glittering facet. Then Jenny had given a low moan. Anna had looked round at her immediately and realised that she was feeling nauseous.

She'd acted instinctively. Pulling back with deliberate clumsiness, she'd dragged on the edge of the bowl and it had tipped over, spilling jewels all over the table.

And some had slithered on to the floor.

She and Jenny—and half a dozen others—had scrambled around on the floor, mostly feeling with their fingers in the sharply delineated shadow under the table on the cold stone flags. While she was down there she'd managed to whisper to Jenny, 'Are you going to be sick? I'll call time and say I need the loo—come with me—'

All the other model had done was to shake her head vigorously and go on searching for bits of jewellery, almost head to head with three security personnel, a dresser, Kate, and one of the photographer's assistants.

Jenny had been the last to stand up, Anna recalled. She'd deposited an emerald ring, a ruby brooch and a sapphire bracelet back into the bowl, while Anna herself had contributed one ruby earring and a diamond choker. As Jenny had got to her feet, Anna, still watching her worriedly, had seen her wince.

I thought it was because she still felt nauseous, but it wasn't. She slipped the ruby bracelet inside her shoe while she was getting to her feet...

That was how she'd done it. Kept it hidden inside her shoe for the rest of the shoot, and then somehow, in the crush of the changing room, she must have transferred it into her sleeve.

Dismay hollowed out again in her. How *could* Jenny have been so insane?

No—no time to think about what had driven her friend to such folly. All that was important now was getting rid of the bracelet in such a way that its temporary disappearance could not be linked to Jenny.

She gained the head of the staircase leading down to the guest level upper floor. From there, the huge main staircase flowed down to the hall. At the top, she paused a moment. Instinctively, she realised, she'd been heading back to the scene of the crime—the main hall, where the huge oaken table sat solidly in its splendour.

Her eyes blinked, even as her stomach flushed with icy water again.

Two of the security guards were systematically working their way along the length of the table on either side, feeling underneath the surface.

Anna watched, frozen with horror. Even as she stood there, unable to move, there was the sound of a vehicle approaching, drawing to a sudden halt, and then, moments later, the huge front door of the Schloss swung open and Leo Makarios walked in.

He was in skiing clothes, Anna registered absently. And he was also, she realised, fully cognisant of the fact that the ruby bracelet was missing.

He strode up to the security guards and barked something at them. Anna saw them shake their heads and then resume their painstaking search. Anna found herself wondering quite what they were doing. Then it came to her.

They must have realised that the only opportunity the thief had had was when the jewels had been spilt. Which meant—

Oh, God, she felt sick—if they thought that, then they could also severely limit the number of suspects.

For one long moment she stared down at Leo Makarios, standing hands on hips, thick skiing jacket pushed back, continuing to watch the guards. His face was expressionless, but his eyes—his eyes made a sick, cold punch go through her. Then, appearing out of the nether regions of the Schloss, she saw his gofer, Justin, come hurrying up to him. His face looked like curd-cheese, and Anna almost felt sorry for him.

But she couldn't think about him now, or the kind of tongue-lashing, and worse, he was about to get from his employer. She had to think of herself—and Jenny.

You can't just stand here—go—move! Clear off!

She jerked back from the balustrade.

It was a mistake.

The movement caught Leo Makarios's eye. His head whipped up from where he was on the receiving end of Justin's agitated discourse.

He saw her instantly.

And in that moment, Anna knew that she would rather die than have him discover the bracelet on her.

She just stood there, frozen. And then, from somewhere, she found a strength of mind she'd never even known she possessed. Slowly, she began to walk down the stairs. A model's walk—almost a saunter.

As she did so, she saw Leo Makarios's eyes narrow. Something leapt in them, and for a second she reeled from it. Then a flood of relief went through her.

She knew that look. And though at any other time she would have felt her hackles rise automatically, now, for the first time in her life, she could have gone down on her knees at being on the receiving end of such a look.

Casually, knowing she absolutely, totally and completely must not—*must not* behave in any way other than utterly ignorant—utterly *innocent*—she kept on walking downstairs.

Think—think! What would you do if you were seeing Leo Makarios for the first time after that scene last night?

But she was, of course. Seeing him for the first time since last night...

And it just so happens—the cold poured through her insides again —*that you currently happen to have his priceless Levantsky ruby bracelet in your pocket.*

For one overwhelming moment Anna felt the urge to just walk up to him, fish the bracelet out of her pocket, and hand it to him with some kind of smartass remark like, *Is this what you're looking for?*

But it was impossible—completely impossible. To reveal she

had it, however innocent she might be as to its original theft, would simply be to condemn Jenny. And she couldn't, *wouldn't* do that. She'd promised herself she would help Jenny get through this ruination of her life, and she would stick by that. Jenny's problems were far too great to have to cope with being accused of theft as well.

So, instead, she had to behave as she would have if she'd had no idea what was going on. As if her only concern was ignoring the man who had almost got her into bed last night.

She reached the bottom of the stairs. Leo was still looking at her, standing stock still. At his side, Justin stood, silenced and cowed. The two security guards were impassively continuing their search.

Anna glanced towards them, a slight frown on her face registering just the right amount of casual curiosity at what they were so inexplicably doing. Then her eyes drifted past them to the tall, threatening figure in the dark skiing jacket.

He was just looking at her. Quite expressionlessly.

Anna's face hardened. For an instant all knowledge of the fact she was walking past him with his stolen bracelet on her person disappeared. All she could see was him, Leo Makarios, who had had the audacity, the *nerve* to think he could turn up in her bedroom at midnight and tumble her over for a quick lay! Sating his carnal appetite on her conveniently available body.

Fury flashed in her eyes—and more than fury.

She kept walking past him.

It was like going through a forcefield, every step.

'One moment.'

Leo's voice was like iron.

She halted. She turned her head towards him. Saying nothing. Just letting that look of scornful anger sit in her eyes. Totally ignoring the sick fear inside her.

'Where are you going?'

Her lips pressed together. 'I'm off duty now, Mr Makarios. So I'm going to get some fresh air.'

Did she sound insolent? She didn't care.

His brows snapped together.

'Without a jacket or boots? In the dark?'

She gave a shrug. It cost her, but she did it.

'Five minutes won't kill me,' she returned indifferently.

She went on heading for the vast wooden doors.

It took every ounce of strength she possessed. Every nerve was screaming. Every muscle tearing. Every step was as if she were walking on glass.

The doors seemed a mile away. If she could just reach them and get outside she would be safe.

Safe outdoors. Safe from Leo Makarios's deadly, *dangerous* regard, with the bracelet safe in her pocket...

She didn't mean to. She really, really didn't mean to. But she could not stop herself. It was an instinct so overpowering that her hand moved of its own accord.

Her fingers brushed along her right thigh, feeling the hidden lumpiness of the rubies. Telling her they were still safe.

She was nearly at the doors. Behind her, she could hear Justin's voice agitatedly resume, presumably telling his employer all the things the security personnel were doing to recover the missing jewellery.

Her hand was reaching out for the iron ring, to turn it and open the door.

Ten more seconds and I'll be outside.

Just hold your nerve. Hold it!

'One moment, if you please, Ms Delane.'

Leo's command was like ice. Cold and very, very hard.

Anna froze.

She stood, quite immobile, her hand still reaching out to open the front door. She did not turn round. Had no power to do so. No power to do anything except stand there with her mind screaming at her.

She heard his heavy-booted footsteps ringing on the stone flags, walking up to her.

'I'd like a word with you.'

She twisted her head round slowly, disdainfully. Claws

crushed at her stomach, but she knew she had to keep her nerve.

What would she do if she were innocent?

She would be uncooperative, rejecting.

Her mouth tightened.

'Yes?' she said stonily.

'In private.' His voice was grim.

Deliberately, Anna stared at him. It was hard, punishingly hard, but she met his eyes. They were completely expressionless, and somehow that frightened her even more than if she had seen that look in them she hated.

'I have nothing to say to you, Mr Makarios,' she said, in a tight, low voice.

His expression did not change.

'I have some questions to ask you.' His voice twisted, and for a second she saw that look flash briefly. 'Be assured it has nothing to do with the subject you so clearly wish to avoid.' He gestured with his hand. 'This way.'

Should she refuse? What would look worse?

If she made too much objection would she draw attention to herself? Arouse suspicions? After all, there was nothing he could know—nothing he could *do*.

Except ask questions she would find—would *have* to find!—innocent answers to.

'Very well,' she said, in a clipped, tight voice.

She marched off in the direction he was indicating. It was to a door on the far side of the hall, and she had no idea where it led. Behind her she could hear Leo Makarios's heavy booted tread ringing on the flags. In her stomach acid pooled; her heart was racing.

Be glad about last night! It's giving you a cover for your obvious tension now!

Anna gritted her teeth. She just had to hold her nerve, that was all.

She stopped outside the room. Leo Makarios opened the door and ushered her in.

It was an office, she saw instantly. Lined with bookshelves and predominantly occupied by a vast desk on which stood a PC.

She walked in and stopped. Then turned around and looked belligerently at Leo Makarios closing the door behind him.

It was not a small room, but as the solid wood door snapped shut it suddenly seemed claustrophobically confined.

'Well?' she demanded. 'What's all this about?'

Her chin lifted, but behind the belligerent expression on her face she could feel herself paling.

Leo was standing there very still, just looking at her.

Quite expressionless.

The dark padded ski jacket made him look even more formidable than he usually looked.

'I would like you, Ms Delane, to empty your pockets.'

The blood drained from her face completely.

With an effort of will she forced an expression of astonishment to her features.

'What?'

He did not move. 'You heard me. Empty your pockets.'

'No!' she retorted indignantly, trying desperately to stay in character. She took a harsh breath. 'What is this? What the hell is going on?'

'You've gone pale, Ms Delane. Even paler than usual. Why is that, I wonder?'

His eyes were resting on her like weights, but she had to keep staring back at him angrily. Not letting her fear show.

But the fear was there, all right—like pickaxes gouging in her stomach.

'Because I don't want to be anywhere near you. That's why! Isn't it obvious, Mr Makarios?' she thrust defiantly at him.

Did his eyes narrow very, very slightly?

'Obvious—or convenient?'

'*What?*'

His mouth tightened.

'Just empty your pockets, please.'

'No, I will not. What the hell is this about?'

'Just do it.'

Anna's expression hardened.

'How dare you harass me like this—?'

Leo Makarios's face suffused with instant thunder. His hand slammed down on to the surface of his desk.

'You will not use that word! *Christos*—' He took a harsh, ripping breath. 'Very well—if you do not wish to empty your pockets, you need not do so.' He moved his hand, picking up the phone. 'You can instead let the police search you.'

'The *police*?' With all her nerve she tried to inject as much withering bewilderment into her voice as she could. 'Are you mad?' she challenged derisively. 'I've had enough of this!'

She turned on her heel and headed for the door.

It was locked. Between fear and fury she rattled the handle viciously. She could no longer tell whether she was still in character as someone totally innocent, or succumbing to an overriding instinct to run and run and run.

'Let me out!'

Footsteps sounded behind her across the carpet. Then Leo Makarios was right behind her.

'Of course,' he said smoothly. His arm came around her to unlock the door.

The other hand slid into her trouser pocket and drew out the bracelet.

He stepped back.

For one endless second Anna froze. Then she twisted round, pressed back against the door panels. Like a deer at bay, cornered by a ravening leopard.

Leo Makarios was just standing there, hand palm up, a river of fire draped over his long fingers. He was so close to her his presence pressed on her like a crushing dark weight.

For a moment he said absolutely nothing, just hung her eyes with his as if he were crucifying her.

Then he spoke.

Each word a nail in her flesh.

'Well, well, well,' he said slowly, and the way he spoke was like acid dripping on her bare skin. 'So the virtuous Ms Delane—so virtuous she won't allow her lily-white breasts to be photographed, so innocent she is outraged by a man's touch on her—all along is nothing but a thief.'

She couldn't move, couldn't think. Could only feel the horror spreading through her like freezing water.

Think! Think—say something. Anything…

But every synapse in her brain was freezing.

She watched him walk back to his desk, lay the bracelet on its surface. Then he turned back to look at her.

Fury flashed across his face. Anger so intense she thought it would slay her where she stood. Then, with monumental effort of will, his face stilled.

Behind her back she could feel the hard panels of the door pressing into her. Nowhere to run; nowhere to hide.

Caught red-handed in possession of stolen property. A ruby bracelet worth untold tens of thousands of pounds!

And the only way to clear her name would be to incriminate Jenny.

I can't! I can't do that! Whatever happens, I've got to keep her out of it!

But even as the resolution went through her she felt fear buckle. It was all very well to say something like that, but if she took the can for appropriating the bracelet it would be *her* the police sirens would sound for, *her* the jail would beckon— and her career would be left in tatters.

Oh God—please, no!

Leo was looking at her, just looking. There was nothing in his face. Nothing at all.

Then, softly, he spoke.

'What shall I do with you? My instinct is to hand you over to the police, to hear the prison doors clang shut on you. And yet…'

He paused. His dark, expressionless eyes rested on her.

Into the silence Anna spoke, each word cut from her. 'What's the point of getting the police involved? You've got the bracelet back. No damage done.'

She was speaking for Jenny; she knew she was. Jenny had acted out of desperation, not greed. Pregnancy did things to you—to your head—and, terrified as Jenny was of the man who had done it to her, the balance of her mind had tipped for a few short, fatal moments. It had been an impulse—desperate, insane—to slip the bracelet into her shoe…

She saw his face change.

'You steal—from me—and think no damage done?' His voice was like a thin, deadly blade.

'Well, there isn't, is there?' She made herself give a shrug. Instinctively she knew she had to hide her fear from him. It would show him her vulnerability, and that was something she must never, never show to Leo Makarios.

Another line of defence came to her, and she lifted her chin defiantly. 'Besides, I can't imagine you'd welcome the publicity that would arrive with the police. You're supposed to be getting *good* publicity from this launch bash—not bad! And it would make your security precautions look pretty pathetic—having some of your precious Levantsky jewels walk off from out under your very nose.'

Even as she spoke she wished she had never said a word. Something was changing in his face again, and it was sending icy fingers down her spine.

He fingered the bracelet, looking across at her, leaning his hips back against the edge of his desk.

'How very astute of you, Ms Delane,' he said. His voice was soft, but it raised the hair on the nape of her neck. 'I would indeed prefer not to make this incident—official. Which is why—' his eyes rested on her '—I am prepared to allow you to make your…reparation…for your crime privately, rather than at the expense of the taxpayer.'

Something crawled in her stomach.

'What—what do you mean?'

'Let's just say…' he answered—and his voice still had an edge in it that was drawing along her skin like a blade— '…that I am giving you a choice. I can hand you over to the police—or I can keep you in *personal* custody until such time as I think you have made sufficient…amends.' His eyes held hers. 'Which is it to be?'

She swallowed. Her heart was thumping in hard, heavy slugs.

'What do you mean?' Her voice was faint. She wanted it to sound defiant, but it didn't.

Leo Makarios smiled. It was the smile of a wolf that had its prey in its clutches. Her stomach clenched. His eyelids swept down over his eyes, the lashes long and lustrous.

'Oh, I think you know, Ms Delane. I think you know.' For a long moment he held her gaze, telling her in that exchange just exactly what he had in mind as reparation.

She felt a shiver go through her.

It was revulsion. It had to be.

It had to be.

A sharp breath rasped in her throat.

'No!' It was instinct—pure survival instinct—that made the word break from her.

He raised an eyebrow.

'No? Are you sure about that, Ms Delane? Have you, I wonder...' his voice was conversational, but it screamed along Anna's nerves '...ever been in prison? You're a very beautiful woman, as you know—exceptionally so. And I'm sure that it isn't just men who find you so. In prison, for example, there will be inmates who—'

'No!'

It was fear this time. Naked and bare.

Just for an instant something showed in Leo Makarios's eyes. Something that did not fit what he was taunting her with. Then it was gone. In its place was merely that cold, scarily level regard.

'No? Then, given the choice, which will you make, hmm?'

Her face convulsed. 'Choice? You're not giving me a choice!'

Anger showed like a flash of lightning in his features.

'You think you deserve one? *Thee mou*, you're a thief! A *thief*. You *stole* from me! You had the audacity, the *stupidity*, to think you could do so with impunity?' His eyes scorched her, as if he would incinerate her on the spot.

Suddenly a Greek word spat from him. He turned, seizing up the phone on his desk, and punched in a number.

'Polizei—'

Anna jerked forward.

'Please—don't! Don't...don't call the police.'

There was panic in her voice. He mustn't involve the police—he mustn't! They would investigate the theft, Jenny would realise she'd been found out—and she'd confess—Anna knew she would.

And the consequences would be unthinkable. The case would hit the press, Jenny's condition would inevitably be exposed in the time it took to come to trial, and when it did she'd lose her baby for ever.

The man who had threatened to take her child from her would arrive to make good his threat. Jenny would lose her freedom and her baby. She'd be branded a criminal and end up in jail, her life ruined, her child taken from her...

And Anna could not let that happen.

Not if there was some way to avoid it.

Slowly, as if from a long distance, she saw Leo Makarios lower the receiver to the handset and turn back to her.

Faintly, forcing her voice to pass her throat, Anna spoke.

'I need to know...know...exactly what would be involved if I agreed to...to the...the reparation you...you spoke of. I mean—how...how long for...and...when? I mean...'

He was looking at her. Something was in his eyes again, and it made her feel cold.

'How long?' he echoed. His voice was silky suddenly. 'Why, Ms Delane—until I've had all I want of you. Or—' there was a note in his voice that shivered down her spine '—until you please me sufficiently to earn your parole. There—is that exact enough for you? Or would you like me to spell out *exactly*—' his repetition of the word mocked her '—how I envisage you earning your parole?'

He was baiting her, taunting her, wanting her to lash out, scream her defiance, her revulsion at him. She could see it, knew it all the way through her.

And she burned to do it! Burned to tell him to take his disgusting sick 'choice' and—

But she couldn't. Couldn't do anything except just stand there and let him say such things to her.

'And...' She swallowed, forcing herself to go on. 'And if I...if I agree, then...then you won't involve the police, or the press, or...anyone else? No one will know except...you?'

His mouth curved in a contemptuous curl.

'No one will know that you are a thief—is that what you mean?'

'Yes.'

She stared at him. It was essential, *essential* that he agreed that. Because somehow she had to keep this from Jenny. Her mind went racing ahead. If she could tell Jenny that she'd safely returned the bracelet, that no one had found out, that it had all gone quiet, she might just save her friend.

What else am I going to have to tell her?

Oh, God, what on earth was she going to say to Jenny? No, she would think about that later. Not now. Not when Leo Makarios was looking at her with a contemptuous expression on his face that would have made her flush with shame if he'd had the cause for it he thought he had.

But he *didn't* have cause. She knew he didn't!

So was that why she lifted her chin and stared back at him defiantly, *refusing* to let herself be cowed, humiliated, ashamed.

She felt her resolve stiffening as she held his coruscating gaze. What did she care what he thought of her? What did she care if he thought her a thief or not? Because she knew *exactly* what she thought about him—a man who'd walked into her bedroom last night in the sublime assumption that she was just going to sigh with gratitude and lie down for him...

No—don't think about that!

Because if she thought then she might remember, and if she remembered then she might...

She might prefer Leo Makarios to phone the police after all...

But she couldn't let him do that.

Oh, God, it was like being crushed between walls closing in on her, closing in—

With a mental strength she hadn't known she possessed she pushed them apart. She could not collapse now—could not panic, or faint, or burst into tears. She had to keep going—keep going with what she had done. So she went on staring at him defiantly, chin high.

She could see it angered him. See it in the flash of blackness in his eyes, and she was darkly, viscously pleased. She knew it was irrational, and certainly stupid, to anger even more a man who had such cause to be furious with her.

And part of her brain told her it was unjust as well.

He thinks you're a thief. He's got a right to be mad with you!

But reason did not hold sway. Somehow keeping Leo Makarios angry with her made her feel safer—safer than Leo Makarios feeling anything else about her...

Or was it?

As Anna stood there, her back pressed against the door, with those heavy-lidded, hard-as-stone eyes boring into her like diamond-tipped drills, a sense of almost overpowering disbelief shuddered through her.

Oh, God, what have I done...?

The words ricocheted round and round inside her head. Like bullets. Each one a killing shot.

But it was too late to do anything now. Far too late. She'd taken on the burden of Jenny's crime and now she had to see it through.

And the only way to do that, she knew, was not to think about it. Absolutely not think about what she had just agreed to.

A barrier sliced down in her brain. Don't think about anything but *now*! That was all she must deal with.

'Well,' she heard her voice say, and marvelled that it sounded so cool, so unconcerned, 'what happens now, then?' She levered herself away from the door panel, deliberately thrusting her hands inside her pockets, staring, chin lifted, across at the man who had caught her red-handed with a price-less ruby bracelet in her illicit possession.

Again her attitude seemed to send a flash of black anger through his eyes.

'What happens now, Ms Delane,' he intoned heavily, with that killing look still levelled at her, 'is that you get out of my sight. Before I change my mind and get you slung into jail, where a thief like you belongs! Now, get out.'

Leo's eyes were dark, inward-looking, his face closed. He could feel the black deadly rage roiling through him like a heavy sea.

How *dared* she think she could steal from him? And then deny it, defy him as she had? *Christos*, he had heard the word *shameless* used before, but never had he realised just what it meant. His face darkened even more. Now he did.

She stood there in front of me, lying through her teeth. Pretending her innocence even as the bracelet was in her pocket.

And she might even have got away with it.

He saw again in his head the moment when she'd headed towards the front door of the Schloss, walking with her elegant, poised model's saunter, distancing herself completely from the search going on behind her.

And all along...

But she'd given herself away. That tiny but instinctive ges-ture she'd made with one hand, brushing her pocket.

Checking if something was still there...

And he'd known—known with every gut instinct—that the thief was her. He'd already carpeted the cowering Justin, lam-basted the head of security for the shambles that had happened that afternoon. It had been obvious that that was when the theft had taken place, and the only suspects had been those close enough to the spilt jewels to have purloined any.

It had been Anna Delane who'd spilt them in the first place. Anna Delane who'd been the first to scrabble down to the ground. Every finger had already been pointing at her.

But investigating would have been a delicate business. The missing bracelet could have been anywhere in the Schloss—secreted in any of a thousand unlikely places for collection later. Or even off the premises. It could have been miles away, in completely different hands. Searching any of the suspects' rooms would have been fruitless.

And Anna Delane had had the audacity to think she could walk straight past him carrying it on her!

The black rage roiled through him again. That anyone should have stolen from *him*—and for it to be her—her of all people.

His eyes narrowed.

Had he been mad to let her walk out? Mad not simply to pick the phone up again and get the police here?

But the vixen had been right. She'd gone immediately for his one weak spot—his determination to avoid any bad publicity tainting the launch of the Levantsky jewels.

No. Leo let his rage sink down again, congealing into a cold, hard mass inside him. He'd done the right thing. No police—no publicity—no prison.

Anna Delane would make amends to him in a manner he would find far, far more satisfying.

She didn't want him in her bed? Thought herself too virtuous for his desires?

A grim smile twisted at his mouth.

She'd be *begging* for him before he was done with her!

CHAPTER FIVE

ANNA sat in her wide leather seat in the first class cabin and stared unseeingly at the glossy magazine lying across her lap. At her side, separated from her only by a drinks table, sat Leo Makarios.

He was working at his laptop, completely ignoring her.

But then, he'd ignored her almost entirely ever since she'd fled from his office, taking on her shoulders the burden of guilt for a crime she had not committed.

Accepting the blame for having stolen a priceless bracelet.

Accepting the 'choice' Leo Makarios had held out to her.

But she hadn't had any other option. She'd told herself that over and over again, like a litany running in her head. She could not let Jenny be sent to prison and have her baby taken from her, brought up in some faraway desert country, where wives were locked up in harems, kow-towing to every male in sight…

So I'm going to have to go through with what Leo Makarios wants. There's nothing else I can do.

Yet the enormity of it crushed her. Appalled her.

She couldn't think about it; she just couldn't. It was the only way she could keep going. By not thinking about what she had done, what she was going to do…

She willed herself not to think. Because if she thought about it, if for a moment, a single moment, she let her brain accept what she had agreed to, she would, she would…

The grille sliced shut in her brain again. Stopping her thinking. Stopping her doing anything—anything at all except what she had to do.

And it had started straight away—last night, when she'd walked out of Leo Makarios's office, with the word *thief* branded on her, to see the person she had taken the branding for.

She'd made herself go back to Jenny's room and tell her that she'd simply slipped the bracelet under the hall table, positioning it such that it was in shadow, obscured by one of the heavy wooden struts supporting the table's weight.

'They'll just think they missed it, that's all,' she'd told Jenny.

Her friend had gone white with relief.

'I must have been insane,' she'd whispered, burying her head in her hands and starting to cry.

Mopping up Jenny had taken all Anna's energies. So had getting through the evening ahead.

A gala ball, followed by fireworks, opened by a breathtaking descent down the grand staircase of all four models *en grande tenue*, glittering, for the last time, with the full panoply of the Levantsky jewels, to the music of Strauss and the audience's applause.

It had taken all Anna's professionalism to get through the evening. Only one thing had been spared her—waltzing with Leo Makarios.

Or, indeed, being anywhere near him. If the previous evening he'd kept her glued to his side, last evening he'd done the opposite. He hadn't danced with any of the models, sticking to high-ranking female guests like the Austrian minister's wife.

Anna had been sickly grateful. And even more grateful to the kindly German spa-loving industrialist who'd made a beeline for her. She'd hung on to him all evening.

When the ball had finally ended, deep in the early hours of the morning, and the models had been let off duty at last, Anna had hurried back to her room.

And locked her door.

If Leo Makarios wanted to come in he'd have to break through it with a sledgehammer.

But he had other plans for her, she'd learnt that morning, after a nerve-racking, sleepless night.

She'd been packing when the knock on her door had

sounded. It had been Justin, pompously informing her of a new assignment.

'Mr Makarios has very generously extended your booking,' he'd told her. 'It's all arranged with your agency. You'll be leaving in an hour. Please do not be late.'

Leaving for where? Anna had wondered.

Now, four hours later, she knew.

She was flying to the Caribbean, with Leo Makarios at her side.

To have as much sex with him as he warranted would atone for stealing the Levantsky rubies from him.

She felt sick all the way through every cell in her body.

Anna hung on to the strap above the door in the car as it bumped over the potholed island roads. She was dog-tired. In the front passenger seat Leo Makarios was talking to the driver, and she was dully grateful that he was continuing to ignore her.

Anna turned her head away, staring out into the black subtropical night. She'd been to the Caribbean before, on fashion shoots, but never to this particular island. At least it had been easy to convince Jenny that that was all this was—an unexpected extra shoot that Leo Makarios wanted done in a subtropical setting. Rich men, both she and Jenny knew, were capricious, and they expected others to jump when they said so.

As for Jenny herself, Anna had phoned mutual friends of theirs—a photographer and his wife—who would meet Jenny at Heathrow. The couple owned a holiday cottage in the Highlands, and had promised to keep Jenny there until Anna got back to the UK.

When that would be, Anna did not want to think.

Or about anything that was going to happen. As she had done every waking hour since that hideous exchange in Leo Makarios's office, Anna shut off her mind.

She kept it shut even when the car arrived at its destination, driving through metalwork gates set in a high retaining wall and along a smooth gravelled drive to draw up in front of a large, low villa. As she got out, the chill of the air-conditioned interior evaporated into the hot sub-tropical night. For a moment she simply stood there, taking in the sounds and smells of the Caribbean, the croaking of the tree frogs and the heady fragrance of exotic blooms.

Then she was following Leo Makarios indoors, back into air-conditioned cool and a huge, cathedral-ceilinged reception room. The light dazzled her. She took in an impression of great height, cool marble floors, lazily circling overhead fans, wooden shutters and upholstered cane furniture.

Leo Makarios seemed to have completely disappeared.

Instead, a middle-aged woman was coming towards her.

'This way, please,' she said, with a dignified gesture to follow her.

Anna fell in behind, her eyes automatically registering the unselfconsciously graceful walk of the woman—a walk that managed to be both indolent and purposeful. By contrast, she felt she was dragging her own body along, clumsy and exhausted.

Sleep—that was all she wanted. All she craved in the world right now.

The room she was shown to was vast. Up a short, shallow flight of stairs, off a broad gallery-style landing. Inside the room another high, wooden cathedral ceiling soared. A huge mahogany four-poster bed, swathed in what looked like ornamental muslin but was, Anna assumed, mosquito netting, dominated the room. Again, although the room was chilled by air-conditioning, a ceiling fan rotated lazily.

'May I get you some refreshment?' the woman was saying. Even as she spoke a porter entered, carrying Anna's suitcase.

She shook her head.

'Thank you—I'm just going to sleep.'

The woman nodded, said something to the porter in local patois, quite incomprehensible to Anna, and then they both left. Anna looked around her blearily. Her eyes automatically went to the vast four-poster bed.

Easily big enough for two.

Not tonight, Mr Makarios, she thought sourly—you'll have to wait.

Five minutes later, clothes stripped, *en suite* bathroom perfunctorily utilised, she was fast asleep.

Leo stood out on his balcony. A half-moon glittered over the palm-fringed bay that curved in front of the villa. The location was superb, the scene in front of him idyllic, tranquil and untouched. He'd bought this place five years ago, yet how often had he been here? Not often enough.

Life seemed to be rushing by him at ever faster speeds.

Leo's mouth twisted. *So little done, so much to do*—some politician had said that, and he could identify with the sentiment.

Another line drifted through his head.

Getting and spending, we lay waste our powers.

He frowned. No politician, the poet who had said that. And no businessman either. Getting and spending was what his whole life was about. It always had been.

But then, he'd always known that his destiny was to do that. To continue with the work his grandfather had begun, rebuilding the Makarios fortunes after they had been lost in the debacle of the Greek expulsion from Asia Minor in the 1920s.

He could hear his grandfather's harsh voice even now, in his head, from when he'd been a boy.

'We had nothing! Nothing! They took it all. Those Turkii. But we will get everything again—everything!'

Rebuilding the Makarios fortune had occupied his grandfather's life, and his father's, and now his too. The Makarios Corporation spread itself wide—property, shipping, finance, investment, and even—Leo thought of his latest contribution to the family's coffers—the ultimate in luxury goods: priceless historic jewellery, and the revival of a name that had been synonymous with Tsarist extravagance.

He gazed out over the moonlit sea, feeling the warmth of the Caribbean night, hearing the soughing of the wind in the palms, the call of the cicadas, and, drowning them out, the yet more incessant calls of the tree frogs.

A thought came to him out of the soft wind, the sweet-fragranced air.

Who needed diamonds and emeralds on a night like this? Or sapphires and rubies? What use were they here, on the silvered beach by the warm sea's edge?

What use are they at all?

Into his head jarred a voice—'They're just carbon crystals...lots of other common crystals are just as beautiful.' Anna Delane's lofty sneer at the Levantsky jewels.

His face hardened.

Hypocrite! She hadn't helped herself to the ruby bracelet because it was beautiful, but because it was worth a fortune.

It had been a mistake thinking about her. He'd spent the last twenty-four hours assiduously putting her out of his mind. Even when she'd spent the flight sitting right next to him he'd refused to think about her, let alone look at her, or speak to her, or in any way acknowledge her existence. Now, fatally, she was there—vividly in his mind.

Desire shot through him, hard and insistent. His hands clenched over the wooden balustrade.

No! Now was not the time nor the hour. Sleep was the priority now—and it would be for her, too. When he took her it would not be like this, on the edge of exhaustion, but in the rich, ripe fullness of all his powers.

He would need all night to enjoy her to the full.

And every night.

Starting tomorrow.

How long would it take him to tire of her?

The hard smile twisted at his mouth.

A lot, lot sooner than it would take her to tire of him.

He would see to that.

Anna walked along the edge of the beach. It was one of those crystalline white sand, palm-fringed crescents that were put into travel brochures to make everyone instantly want to go there.

But this beach she had to herself. Completely to herself. It belonged to the beautiful sprawling villa spilling along the shore, and the villa belonged to Leo Makarios.

She could see why he'd bought it.

It was, quite simply, idyllic. Like the beach, a travel agent's dream of what a Caribbean villa should look like. The green tiled roof, the white walls, the wraparound veranda, the palm trees fringing the shore, the crystal beach, the pink and purple bougainvillaea and hibiscus splashing colour, the turquoise glitter of a freshwater pool.

Quite, quite idyllic.

Anna stopped to look out to sea. The sun was lowering, a thin band of cloud just above the surface of the sea starting to pool in the lengthening rays of the sun, like rich dye running into spun silk. Bars of gold were sliding across the azure water. Across the sun's face a large, ungainly pelican flapped lazily. High in the sky a frigate bird soared.

Anna glanced at her watch. Though only just evening, the sub-tropical latitudes meant the sun was going down apace. The night would sweep in from the east like a velvet concealing cloak.

And the night would bring, she knew, Leo Makarios.

There had been no sign of him all day. She'd slept long and when she'd surfaced it had been late morning. She'd eaten breakfast on her balcony, and as she'd gazed out over the beautiful grounds leading down to the sea she'd felt the biting, mocking irony of her situation. Here she was in a Caribbean idyll—and tonight she was going to have sex with a man. Deliberate, cold-blooded sex, with a man she did not want to have sex with—a man who thought her a thief, a man she had already thrown out of her bedroom once but who now she could not throw out.

Deliberate, cold-blooded sex.

She made herself say the words again in her head. And again.

Because that was what it was going to be.

Something flared briefly in the depths of her eyes, but she crushed it instantly.

A sudden panic speared through her. She couldn't go through with this. She just couldn't!

I've got to tell him the truth! Tell him it wasn't me who stole his precious bracelet, that it was Jenny, and that she only did it because she's pregnant and terrified, and has got herself involved with a man so dangerous he makes Leo-Money-Bags-Makarios look like a pussycat...

Cold pooled in her stomach. However much she desperately wanted to, she knew she could not tell Leo Makarios the truth. The risks were far too great. As a woman, she might automatically side with Jenny, but who knew what a rich, powerful man like Leo Makarios would think? His attitude to women was dire—she had personal proof of that already—so why should he think Jenny deserved any favours, any mercy? After what she'd heard him say about Vanessa, and guarding his precious cousin from her, he'd probably think Jenny had got herself pregnant on purpose—picking a rich man to get at his money—and that a man so entrapped was entitled to take a woman's baby from her—especially a woman who'd shown herself so morally lax that she'd stooped to theft... He wouldn't understand.

No—Anna's face closed—there was no way she could take that risk. And that meant—her expression twisted—she just couldn't tell Leo Makarios why she had taken the blame for stealing his rubies.

He had to go on thinking that *she* was the thief. It was the only way she could protect Jenny.

Which meant—the fear pooled in her stomach again, but with a different cause this time—that she was, indeed, going to have to go through with what Leo Makarios intended.

Have sex with him.

She stared unseeingly out over the water. In Austria it had seemed unreal; she'd been in shock, Anna realised, using all her mental energy to tamp down the panic that had been trying to erupt. Here, after being on her own all day, the reality of what she was going to have to do was hitting.

Hitting hard.

For a moment she felt revulsion stiffen through her.

A phrase welled up in her thoughts.

Self-respect. An alien concept to so many people, she knew, moving in the world she did. Men who treated women's bodies as commodities—women who treated them the same way. She could name half a dozen other models she knew who would have thought themselves in paradise to have been offered the choice that Leo Makarios had offered. Queued round the block for it.

I'm not one of them!

Even as she mentally shouted her denial, another voice spoke in her head. With killing, merciless force.

But you will be…

Leo Makarios will reduce you to exactly that. Strip you of every last vestige of your self-respect even as he strips the clothes from your body…

Pincers bit inside her stomach, sharp and painful.

She went on staring out over the darkening sea, her mind even darker.

Facing up to what she was going to do.

What she was going to lose.

Yet, for all that was true, she could not sacrifice her friend's future, her baby, just to protect her own self-respect.

I have to do this.

And after all, she thought, with savage mockery at her own prurience, supposing it was Jenny or jail? What would you do then? Would you still stand by her if it meant losing years of your life?

Instead of just a few days…a few nights…

So why make such a fuss about what Leo Makarios is offering?

Even as Anna let the thought into her mind she tried to suppress it.

Leo Makarios was dangerous. She'd thought him so the very

first time she'd set eyes on him, and every encounter with him had proved it to her. Especially the one in her bedroom...

Memory flooded back like a drowning tide, and suddenly she was there, there again, as Leo Makarios held her, kissed her, caressed her—a sensual onslaught that had simply overwhelmed her, made it impossible for her to resist...

Until, with a strength she'd hardly been able to summon, she had flung him from her...

She shut her eyes in anguish, blocking out memory.

Self-respect? The words stabbed at her. Mocking her. Taunting her.

She wasn't just going to sacrifice her self-respect by having deliberate, cold-blooded sex with Leo Makarios. She was going to lose it for a much, much worse reason...

She turned away abruptly. Grimly, she headed back up the beach in the brief sub-tropical dusk.

Her face had hardened.

She couldn't get out of it now. That wasn't in her power. Not if she wanted to keep Jenny safe, herself out of jail.

But she could, she *must* ensure that it was nothing but deliberate, cold-blooded sex.

Nothing more.

Dear God, let me have the strength I need—please, please!

'More champagne?'

'No, thank you.'

'Smoked salmon?'

'No, thank you.'

'Caviar?'

'No, thank you.'

'As you wish.' There was an amused, baiting quality to Leo's voice. He sat back in his rattan chair on the terrace. From the veranda the gardens were landscaped so that the curve of the beach opened up, framed by palm trees. A light, cooling breeze came off the sea. Moonlight bathed the surface of the water.

It was a beautiful scene—and the woman sitting opposite

him complemented it perfectly. His eyes slid over her as she sat there, ramrod-straight, staring determinedly out to sea.

She was wearing a jade-green loose silk-trousered affair, with long sleeves and a high collar. As she'd stalked across the terrace, her hair caught back in a stark, high knot, not a scrap of make-up on her, he'd read the signals coming from her as if she'd been broadcasting in neon.

She was making not the slightest attempt to look alluring.

It hadn't worked in the least. Anna Delane would have looked alluring in a sack. Her body had a long-limbed grace that could not be disguised, and the bones of her face had been constructed with a natural artistry that meant make-up or hair-style was an irrelevance.

Oh, yes, Anna Delane had an allure that she could not suppress. Leo gave a mocking, inward smile. Even when she was doing her best to be sullen and monosyllabic, as she was now.

He took a mouthful of champagne and contemplated her. A sliver of irritation wormed its way under his amusement. She really was a piece of work—sitting there as stiff as a board and twice as hostile. He'd caught her red-handed, a proven thief. But was she abashed? Guilty? Contrite?

The words were unknown to her, clearly.

Shameless. That was the only word that fitted her.

He took another mouthful of champagne and washed off the irritation. Well, there was an expression in English that perfectly captured Ms Anna Delane's forthcoming fate—riding for a fall.

And she would do it, very, very satisfyingly, in his bed.

Anticipation eased through him. He was going to enjoy Anna Delane, every last exquisite drop of her—and the greatest enjoyment would be her enjoyment of him. However galling it was to her.

He reached out a hand and scooped some more beluga with his spoon.

Numbly, Anna took another forkful of grilled fish. Somewhere in her mind she knew it was delicious, but it didn't register.

Nothing registered. She wouldn't let it. Must not. Instead she just sat there, eating grilled fish and salad like an automaton, without will or feeling. Resolutely refusing to look at the man sitting opposite her.

He'd abandoned attempts at talking to her, and she was glad. It allowed her to keep her mind blank—as blank as her expression. She was well trained in that—it was like having to stalk out onto a runway, features immobile, not a person at all, just an ambulatory clothes-horse, walking, posing, stopping, going, all at the direction of other people. No will of their own.

Just as she now had no will of her own.

She set her fork aside, having consumed enough. She reached for her champagne and took a small, measured sip, then set her glass back. She'd contemplated getting drunk, but decided against it. Alcohol lowered your guard. Made you stupid. Weak.

And weakness was something she must not allow.

It was far, far too dangerous.

She'd known it, known it with a hollowing of her insides, as she'd walked out on to the terrace this evening.

And set eyes on Leo Makarios again.

A jolt had gone through her that had been terrifying in its intensity. A jolt that had nothing to do with him thinking her a thief and everything to do with the sudden, instant quickening of the blood in her veins, the surge of emotion dissolving through her, the debilitating weakening of her knees.

She'd taken in the presence of Leo Makarios.

Waiting for her.

And almost, almost, she had turned and run.

But she'd forced herself to go forward. She couldn't run. There was nowhere to run to.

So she'd steeled herself, drained all expression from her face, all feeling from her mind, sat herself down and stared out to sea.

Not looking at Leo Makarios. Not looking where he sat, lounging back with lazy, dangerous grace, the open collar of his shirt revealing the strong column of his throat, the turned-up cuffs showing the lean strength of his wrist and hands, the taut material over his torso emphasising the breadth of his chest.

And not looking, above all, at his face. The wide, sensual mouth, the dark heavy-lidded eyes.

Eyes that pressed on her like weights.

With all her strength she sat there, impassive, indifferent, while her stomach contorted in hard, convoluted knots.

Praying for the strength to get through the ordeal ahead.

But she could not, dared not, put into words what she was praying for.

The meal seemed to go on for ever. She refused dessert, desultorily picking at a slice of mango and sipping mineral water, her champagne abandoned. Leo Makarios, it seemed, was in no hurry. He'd eaten a leisurely first course, a leisurely main course, and had made a considered selection from the cheese board.

Finally he leant back, brandy swirling slowly in his glass, a cup of coffee at his place, eyes resting on her contemplatively.

'Tell me something,' he said suddenly, his tone conversational. 'Why did you steal the bracelet?'

Anna's head turned. Her eyes looked at him, widening slightly as the meaning of what he'd just asked registered. The question seemed extraordinary.

'That's none of your business,' she returned repressively.

For a moment Leo Makarios just stared at her, as if he did not believe what she'd just said. Then a thread of anger flashed in his eyes. Next it was gone.

He leant back in his chair and gave a laugh.

It was an incredulous, disbelieving laugh, with not the slightest trace of humour in it.

'You really are a piece of work,' he said slowly. His eyes narrowed slightly. 'Aren't you going to tell me it was for your sick grandmother, or something? To pay for an operation?' His voice was jibing.

She looked at him levelly. 'No.' Her voice was expressionless, but inside emotion was running. Thank God she had not

tried to throw herself and Jenny on his mercy—his taunt just
now showed exactly how he'd have received her plea. No. Her
face hardened. There was only one way out of this, and that
was the way Leo Makarios had given her in his office.

Oh, God, just let it be over and done with!

She just wanted it over and done with. That was all she
wanted.

Suddenly, tension spilling out of her in words, she spoke.

'Look, what's with this stupid inquisition? You gave me the
choice of the police or you—and here I am. So what are you
waiting for? You've had your dinner—why hang around? Just
get it over and damn well done with!'

Her voice was terse.

For a moment he just went on looking at her, his face suddenly unreadable. Then, abruptly, he set down his brandy and
got to his feet.

'Very well. Time for bed, Ms Delane. Let the reparation
begin.'

Was there mockery in his words? She couldn't tell. Didn't
know.

Didn't care.

This was it, then. No more tense, fraught waiting. No more
prevarication.

She was going to go to bed with Leo Makarios.

Right now. Now.

And have sex with him.

Carefully Anna got to her feet. Her heart, she could tell,
seemed to have gone strangely numb as well. Just like the rest
of her.

She could only be grateful.

It was the best way to get it over and done with.

She just had to keep her nerve, that was all. Endure. Let him
take what he wanted and it would be over.

At least for now. Tomorrow night she'd have to go through
it all again, but that was tomorrow. She'd think about that then.
Now she just had to focus on getting through tonight.

She walked into the villa ahead of him, every footstep, his

and hers, falling heavily on the marble floor, and let him guide her up the shallow flight of stairs into a room that was not hers.

His, evidently.

She stood for a moment in the middle, not sure what to do. There was a large bed in here, just like in her bedroom, but this one was not a four-poster, and it did not have yards of muslin draped. The air was cool from the air-conditioning, but not as chilly as the setting in her room. On either side of the bed low lamps provided the only illumination, making the room shadowed, intimate.

'Wait there.'

She did as she was told. Leo Makarios disappeared into his *en suite* bathroom. She heard the sound of water running. Anna went on standing there, immobile. Her brain was frozen, her mind empty. She couldn't think, couldn't feel. She was standing in Leo Makarios's bedroom, waiting for him to emerge from his bathroom and take her to his bed. It was impossible, outrageous.

And yet it was happening.

Now.

Tonight.

She should be feeling something, she knew—but she felt nothing. Nothing at all.

Only the hard, heavy thumping of her heart in her breast, the tautness in the line of her jaw told her that, numb though her mind was, her body was registering the anxiety, the tension in her psyche at what was going to happen.

Tonight.

Now.

She went on standing there. Not looking. Not thinking. Not feeling.

Completely numb.

The bathroom door clicked open and Leo Makarios reappeared. He was wearing a white towelling robe. Short. To the knees. Belted tight. The whiteness made his Mediterranean skin tone even darker in the subdued lamplight.

Anna felt some kind of emotion prickle out across her skin.

She watched him as, scarcely glancing at her, he went across to the bed, drew back the covers, and lounged down against the pillows, propping them up behind him. His long tanned legs stretched out bare on the white sheets.

He settled his gaze on her.

Time seemed to stop. Stop completely. As if the world had stopped turning.

His eyes were dark, unreadable. His face immobile.

But something in his eyes made the prickling intensify across her skin.

A pressure started to build.

Inside her—outside her. In the room, in the space between where she was standing, motionless, numb, in the middle of Leo Makarios's bedroom, and where he was lounging back on his bed.

Looking at her.

Waiting for her.

For one endless moment the silence held.

Then he spoke.

'Come here,' he said softly.

For the space of a single heartbeat—which lasted an unbearable agony of time—Anna did not move.

Could not move.

Somewhere deep in her head words were forming. She could hear them, very low. They were telling her to run. To yell. To shout abuse at the man who lounged back against his pillows like some eastern pasha, waiting for his slave woman to come and pleasure him...

But even as she heard the muffled, vehement words they were stifled. Extinguished.

She could not listen to their siren call. Must not.

If she did, Jenny would be doomed.

Slowly, like a puppet, Anna started walking towards him. Feeling nothing, she stood beside the bed.

Docile. Compliant to his will.

Holding down with iron force the voice that was trying to

speak deep inside her head. The pressure that was building, molecule by molecule, inside her veins.

It wanted to get out, she knew. She must not allow it.

Must not.

She went on standing there, motionless beside Leo Makarios's bed, with him lounging back against the headrest.

Looking at her.

There was something in his eyes, dark and hooded, something that made the prickling in her skin intensify again, as if the voltage applied to her flesh had just been increased.

She felt her breath quicken and tried to suppress it.

His eyes washed over her.

Her heart started to slug in her chest; her veins dilated.

Desperately she tamped it down.

Leo's voice was murmuring. Slow, and low, with a creamy, sensual timbre.

'Oh, Anna Delane, you have no idea how much I'm going to enjoy this.'

His voice was soft and heavy. His eyes slumberous with desire.

He reached a hand out to her, taking hers in his. Her hand was limp, inert.

He drew her down on the bed and she sat there, half twisted towards him. Looking at him. Nothing in her eyes. Nothing at all.

She was a doll, a puppet. Capable of no feeling at all...

Slowly, never taking his dark, slumberous eyes from her, he lifted his hands to her hair, pulling out the pins. Her long black hair tumbled down over her shoulders, cascading over the jade-green silk.

Leo spoke again, his Greek accent low and heavy, his lashes sweeping down over those dark golden eyes.

'You come to me like a sacrificial virgin.' His hands sifted through her hair. 'Laying down your virtue for me. Pure, unsullied, innocent.' Something shifted in the depths of those eyes. Shifted, and hardened.

Like his voice.

'How extraordinarily deceptive appearances can be.'

The words drawled from him.

She did not respond. Did not speak. Did not do anything except go on sitting there as his long, sensual fingers sifted through her hair. Her body was like marble—motionless, insensate. It had to be—it had to be—she must not be anything else! Must not let herself feel his fingers in her hair, feel the myriad pressure points in her skull sending a soft, shivering sensation through her. She must not feel that.

Must remember she was only a puppet. Feeling nothing. Nothing at all.

His fingers stopped, then slid through her hair to stroke the back of her neck. Slowly, sensually...

And suddenly, out of nowhere, sensation started to flow through her. She tried to stop it, tried to remember why she was there, with no feelings, no thoughts, no will, merely a mindless doll that Leo Makarios could touch and stroke, and she would let him, because that was what she had to do...

But it was impossible.

She could not stop herself. Could not stop the sensation rippling through her as his fingers played with the sensitive skin they were touching.

She felt her eyes close. Heavy, slumberous.

Slowly, his fingers tautened around her nape. Leisurely he drew her down towards him. She let him do it. She let him brush her lips with his, slide his tongue within and start to caress her.

She let him slip her top from her, the silky material sliding away, let him pull her over him, let her bared, braless breasts graze against the towelling of his bathrobe, let his hands slide beneath the waistband of her silk trousers, mould over the soft roundness of her bottom. Even as he started to slide off the material, down her thighs she let him do it, wanted him to.

Anna let him go on kissing her, moving his mouth on hers, let the hard shaft of his manhood probe at the juncture of her legs, let his hand palm her breast in slow, rhythmic circles as its peak ripened under his touch.

She let herself lie there, spread across him. His hand was at the nape of her neck, the other at her breast, and his mouth was on hers, his thighs hard beneath hers, his shaft strong and seeking.

She had no will, no emotion, only total, absolute submission to sensation—sensation he was arousing from her, stroking from her, caressing from her. A slow, spreading fire started to lick through her. A long, low pulse started in her veins, and in every cell of her body a warm, dissolving heat began to steal.

She felt herself move, press her body along his, felt the hardness of his hips, the lean strength of his smooth, muscled chest. Felt her mouth move, move over his, felt herself start to kiss him back, to seek his tongue with hers. Felt the hunger start, deep, deep within her. Felt her hands curl over his strong, sculpted shoulders, revelling in the touch of his skin beneath her kneading fingers.

The fire was licking now, like flames at dry grass, spreading through her veins. She could hear low, aching moans, and knew they were coming from her throat, but she could not stop them. She had no will, no power.

Something had taken her over. Consumed her so completely, so absolutely, she was helpless in its thrall, in its overpowering, overwhelming need.

A need to move her body over his, touching, seeking, questing, with her thighs tautening, hips lifting slightly, so slightly, but just enough, just enough...

She wanted...

She wanted...

She wanted to feel his hand on her breast, palming it, scissoring rhythmically, pulling at her inflamed, jutting nipple. Wanted the other breast to feel the same. Wanted more, more—much more.

The fire was coursing through her, hungry for more to feed it with. The low, aching moans were coming again, need and ravening hunger.

Hunger for him. For the lean, hard body beneath her. For the silky moistness of his mouth, the sensuous gliding of his tongue, the rich velvet of his lips. But it wasn't enough. It wasn't enough.

Fire licked again, all through her veins, but with a new focus, a new urgent source of heat.

She wanted...

She wanted...

She twisted her hips, feeling the long hardness of his shaft at her belly.

She wanted...needed...

Again she lifted her hips, straining down on him with her thighs, her hands pressing on his shoulders, her breast ripe in his hand, as she writhed against his body.

She felt the tip of his shaft against her, and the fire flamed within her. She reared up, hands pinioning his shoulders, her thighs over his, hair tumbling over her back. And with a last, low, rasping moan in her throat she caught his tip at the vee of her legs, lifting and positioning it just where it had to—*had* to be.

He let go her mouth, let go her nape, and she threw back her head, rearing up over him. Her eyes were blind, shut, her body one single writhing twist of flame.

His hand glided down her back in a single smooth sweep, splaying over her bottom.

Words came from him. She could not hear them. Could only feel the tip of his probing shaft at the entrance to her inflamed, aching, flooding body.

And she wanted it. Needed it so much that not having it was a torment, a hunger, a desperation.

So she took it.

Took him into her.

His hand splaying across her guided her down on him, slowly, infinitely slowly, and he filled her, stretching and moulding her.

A long, low exhalation breathed from her. He was solid inside her. Solid, and hard and full. For a long, timeless moment she just stayed there, half-reared over him, feeling his fullness inside her, filling her, filling her so completely that she could only stay completely, absolutely still.

Then slowly, very, very slowly, she moved. Indenting her hips, pressing forward.

And the fire inside her sheeted into flame. White hot flame.

A cry came from Anna as her head fell back, helpless, rolling. She cried out again.

'Is that good?' Leo's voice was low. His hand pressed at her, the fingers at her nipple scything her, sending shoots of pleasure through her. 'Because for me it's good. But this—*this* would be better.'

In a single powerful movement he thrust up into her, and the fire sheeted again, burning down through her hands, her feet. She cried out in pleasure again, louder, more helpless.

He thrust again—up, up into her—and there was a place somewhere, somewhere inside her, that was catching fire, and she wanted...

His hand was on her bottom now, kneading and pressing. He thrust again, and the sensation was unbearable. But he thrust again, and her body was melting, and writhing, and burning.

He thrust again. And this time as he thrust she twisted on him with her hips, and again. The rhythm mounted and mounted, and the fire inside her grew hotter and hotter. More cries were coming from her throat, her body one single flame of sensation, and her head was rolling, rolling. She had become a writhing, ravening hunger, and she wanted...needed...

This.

Oh, God, this—this was what she needed!

The place deep within her, which his thrusting fullness had been stoking, stroking, had caught fire. Igniting in a single blazing funnel of sensation, of pleasure so intense, so consuming, that Anna could not breathe, could only gasp.

And then there was another cry, hoarse and urgent, and Leo was thrusting up into her again. Short, rapid thrusts. His hands suddenly on her shoulders, as he jerked powerfully, repeatedly into her, to reap his own unstoppable pleasure.

She collapsed down on him, panting, exhausted, drained. The storm of sensation shaking her even in its dying embers.

She felt a hand smoothing back the hair from her forehead, felt warm breath on her cheek.

'*Thee mou*, I knew you would be good, but—'

His hoarse voice changed to Greek. It seemed to be coming from a long, long way away. Everything was coming from a distance.

Except for one thing. Something black and dark was rolling in, darker than anything she had ever known. Stifling her, annihilating her.

Slaying her.

It was the realisation of what she had just let happen.

The worst thing in the world...

CHAPTER SIX

LEO strolled out onto his balcony. The sun was high already, and he was not surprised. It had been a long, long night—but very little sleep had taken place.

He stretched in a pleasurable flexing of his shoulders.

Thee mou, but it had been good! More than that—it had been mind-blowing.

And not just for him. Anna Delane had responded exactly as he had known she would.

She'd gone up in flames.

White-hot, scorching flames.

Again and again—all through the night. Time after time he had taken her, and every time he had drawn from her a response that had had her body shaking, shuddering, had her crying out helplessly, reducing her time after time to exhausted, breathless satiation. She had threshed in his arms, her spine arching, hair wild like a maenad, eyes blind and unseeing as she'd convulsed in the extremity of pleasure, totally, completely possessed by it.

It had been intoxicating.

And incredibly arousing.

There had been something exquisitely satisfying about her helplessly sensual response to his touch. She had not intended it, that was for sure. She'd tried to hold back from him, to be like a statue, a block of wood—rigid and unresponsive. But he'd ignored her sullenness, her obvious determination to cheat him of what he wanted from her. Of what she owed him.

He'd got what he wanted from her, all right. Had drawn it from her stroke by stroke, touch by touch, kiss by kiss. Caressing her body with his until she was hot in his arms,

97

giving those low little moans in her throat, moving her body on his in helpless, hungry desire...

He felt his body stir. Even though it had been sated time after time on hers. He gave a low laugh. Time enough to indulge—he was going to be here for as long as he wanted Anna Delane, for as long as she still fed his appetite for her—but right now there was another appetite he wanted to feed. It had been a long time since dinner the night before.

He walked inside the bedroom, picked up the house phone by his bed, and gave his order for breakfast. As he replaced the receiver he let his eyes rest on the woman sleeping in his bed.

She really was extraordinarily beautiful—and never more so than now. Her black hair streamed over the pillow, tumbled and tangled. Her skin was white against the white sheets, black lashes splashing on her cheeks. She was breathing softly.

He gazed down at her.

There was something strangely vulnerable about her.

He frowned slightly.

Vulnerable?

That was the last word he should apply to Anna Delane. Even when he hadn't even known her for a thief she'd radiated attitude. Sharp-tongued, difficult—a troublemaker.

And a hypocrite. Oh, yes. His eyes narrowed. A fully paid-up hypocrite! He'd known from the moment he'd laid eyes on her, when she'd met his look, that she was sexually responsive to him. She'd made no secret of it at all as he'd looked her over and signalled to her that he liked what he saw. And she'd signalled back her response to him clearly enough, all the way through that evening when he'd kept her at his side. Hell, what did she think he'd done that for? Obviously it had been to tell her that he was sexually interested in her. And yet when he'd moved in on that response she'd turned on him like a harpy. Even though she'd been halfway to bed with him when she'd done so.

And then, *then* to subject him to a tirade of virtuous outrage as if she'd never melted like warm honey in his arms—when all along…all along, she'd been nothing but a thief. Daring to steal from him—and making the Levantsky jewels her target. A thief without any sense of shame, or guilt, or contrition. A cool, conscienceless, self-seeking, thieving piece!

But she hadn't been cool when he'd been inside her, when she'd been crying out, threshing in orgasm. She hadn't been cool when he'd held her afterwards, her body shaking, convulsing in the aftermath, her hair tangled, her brow sweated, her breathing rapid and shallow, her heart beating like a frantic bird beneath her ribs.

No, she hadn't been cool then…

He turned away and headed for the *en suite* bathroom. Gazing down at Anna Delane and remembering how she'd been in his arms a few short hours ago was not a good idea right now. He wanted breakfast—time enough for more sex later.

A lot more sex.

He hadn't had nearly enough of Anna Delane yet—she had a *whole* lot more to make up for before he'd be done with her.

'Would you like to swim?'

'No, thank you.'

'Take the catamaran out? Or the launch?'

'No, thank you.'

'Do you want to see the rest of the island?'

'No, thank you.'

'As you wish.'

There was no baiting amusement in Leo's curt voice now. Merely mounting irritation. He picked up his coffee cup and drank, then set it down again. His eyes rested on the woman sitting opposite him.

She was reading a book. A thick paperback that was absorbing all her attention. But then everything and anything absorbed her attention except him. Of him she took no notice whatsoever. She was shutting him out of her existence. She never looked at him, or met his eye, or talked in anything other than the briefest, tersest replies.

She'd been like that since he'd sent for her.

The fact that he'd had to do so had been a source of irritation in itself. He'd come out of his shower to find his bed empty. She'd simply disappeared. It hadn't bothered him. He'd assumed she'd merely gone back to her own room to shower and dress.

But she still hadn't appeared even when he'd despatched one of the staff to tell her that breakfast would be on the terrace. He'd eaten on his own, then sent for her again.

That time she'd come down.

And had stalked stiff-backed across to the table just as she had done the night before. As if she'd never spent the night in his bed.

She'd been wearing dark glasses, completely concealing her eyes. Dark glasses, and her hair back in its punishing knot, and wearing tight black leggings and a long-sleeved sweat top. Completely inappropriate for a hot tropical day.

She'd sat down, totally ignoring him, and turned instead to the maid, requesting a pot of hot water and some fruit.

Then she'd twisted her chair slightly towards the sea view, crossed her long legs, opened her book and started reading.

He might not have been there.

For a minute Leo had looked at her, disbelievingly.

Then he'd spoken.

'*Kalimera*, Anna,' he'd said, in a studied tone.

She'd ignored him.

'Are you always unsociable in the mornings?' His tone had been even more studied.

No answer.

'Anna—'

There had been an edge in his voice then.

She'd turned her head towards him.

He'd been unable to see her eyes. The dark glasses were very effective.

Irritatingly so.

'Yes?'

Her tone had been quelling.

'Tell me—' he'd kept his tone light, civil '—what would you like to do today?'

'Nothing, thank you.'

'There must be something you would like to do,' he'd persisted, with punishing politeness.

But she'd said, 'No, thank you.' In the same tone of complete indifference. And she'd gone on doing so to everything he'd suggested.

Now he just sat here, glaring at her, her nose still buried in her book.

Every last vestige of Leo's good mood vanished.

The maid came out again, placing the requested items on the table. Anna lifted her head out of her book briefly and smiled her thanks. A brief smile, but a smile all the same.

Leo was pretty sure it was the first smile he'd ever seen from her.

It did something strange to him.

He pushed the strangeness aside, watching as she took a teabag from where she'd been using it as bookmark, placed it in a teacup and poured fresh hot water over it. A tangy, herbal scent came off it as it infused.

'Do you not drink coffee?' he asked.

'Very seldom.' She picked up a teaspoon and poked the teabag.

Then she forked a slice of fresh pineapple and placed it on her plate. She started cutting it up, lifting small slices to her mouth.

Silently, Leo slid the basket of fresh breads across to her.

'No, thank you,' she said.

'Are you on a diet?' he enquired.

'I'm always on a diet,' she answered, continuing with her pineapple.

'You hardly need to lose weight.' His eyes ran over her slim, elegant body.

She turned her head to him then.

'That's because I'm always on a diet,' she replied caustically.

She went back to eating her pineapple, then took two slices of papaya, ate those, and pushed her plate away.

'What would you like to eat next?' Leo enquired with punishing civility.

'Nothing, thank you.' She picked up her teacup and took a small sip of the hot herbal tea. Then she placed it back on its saucer and resumed reading.

Leo looked at her fulminatingly.

What the hell was she playing at? Pretending last night had never happened? Pretending she'd never cried out, eyes distended with passion, hands clutching at him, shuddering with orgasm in his embrace?

Evidently, yes.

He stared at her balefully. Hell, she should be purring by now! Her body languorous and sensual from its sating last night. She should have undulated towards him wearing something skimpy, like a bikini with a chiffon sarong caressing her hips, wafting up to him, hair cascading down her back, mouth beestung. She should have leant down, draping her arms around his shoulders, murmuring amorously to him, lowering her mouth to his to greet him…

Instead she was sitting ramrod-straight, answering in terse, caustic monosyllables or totally ignoring him.

Christos, who the hell was she to ignore him? Did she really think she'd prefer a police cell to his bed? Obviously not, or she wouldn't have accepted the bargain he'd offered her. She wanted to save her precious skin, all right, and she hadn't been fussy about how she was going to do that. Well—he glared at her—she could damn well earn her parole, just the way he'd told her when he'd caught her red-handed with his rubies.

By working very, very hard to please him.

He took a mouthful of coffee and then pushed the cup away.

'Anna—'

The edge was back in his voice.

She looked up.

'Yes?'

He rested his eyes on her. For a moment he said nothing.

He thought he saw something flicker in her face, then it was gone.

'Lose the attitude,' he said softly. 'If you'd rather go back to a police cell in Austria, you only have to say. But if you don't, then I suggest you remember what you are here to do, hmm?'

Something changed in her face then, all right. It seemed to blanch even whiter than its usual paleness. Then it was gone again. She set her book down.

'You want sex again?'

The question was delivered in such a deadpan voice that Leo just stared. Distaste knifed through him.

'Spare me your crudities,' he said coldly.

The look came in her face again, then disappeared.

'Well, what do you want, then?' she demanded.

There was belligerence in her voice. It set Leo's back up.

'You can start,' he said tersely, 'with some civility.'

A choke sounded from her.

'Civility?' She echoed the word as if he'd said *DIY brain surgery.*

Leo's mouth tightened.

'We will be here together for at least three weeks—I have no intention of putting up with your ill-humour for that duration.'

She seemed to have gone pale again.

'Three weeks?' she echoed faintly. 'I can't stay here that long!'

Anger shot through him again.

'You think your time in jail would be less?' he riposted sarcastically.

'I've got assignments booked.'

'I will have them cancelled.'

She leant forward.

'No, you will not. I will not have my professional reputation compromised by you high-handedly cancelling my assignments!'

Once more Leo was reduced to just staring at her.

'Your…professional…reputation…?' he echoed. 'I don't believe I just heard you say that! You, Anna Delane, are a *thief*! You have committed a criminal act. I could have you slung in jail. And you dare, *dare* to talk to me of your "professional reputation"?'

Leo pushed his chair back and stood up, his hand slashing through the air.

'Enough! I don't want to hear one more insolent word from you.' He relapsed into Greek, and vented his feelings in several choice expletives. Then he stalked away, his mood as black as thunder.

Behind him, Anna Delane sat very, very still.

She wouldn't crack. She wouldn't. She would not give him that satisfaction.

Satisfaction.

The word jibed at her with cruel taunting. She could still see it now, etched on her memory, the triumphant *satisfaction* on his face as she'd opened her eyes to look down at the man who had just done what he had to her.

Self-hatred lacerated through her. How *could* she have betrayed herself like that? How could she have responded to him, been stroked and caressed and kissed into arousal as she had let herself be?

Until she was helpless, mindless, beyond all control, all salvation.

Beyond anything except the fire that had swept through her body, flamed it to an ecstasy that she had never known existed.

Nothing had ever been like this—nothing.

It had been incredible, ecstatic, exquisite—a stormfire of sensation that had burnt her flesh to the core in a sensual pleasure so intense she had not known it was possible to exist.

I never knew—I never knew it could be like this…

And in that same moment of exultant realisation she had known exactly why she so feared Leo Makarios—just why he was so dangerous to her. She had opened her eyes and realised, with a sickening, ravening horror, what she had done, what she had let him do. What she had *wanted* him to do!

And he had known it. Wanted her to want it, and what he could make her feel. She had seen the triumph in his eyes.

Self-hatred lashed through her again.

Oh, God, she'd walked to his bed like an ignorant, arrogant fool! Thinking she could stay detached, controlled. Uninvolved with what was going to happen to her. She had prayed for strength, but she had been weak—devastatingly, sickeningly weak.

So pathetically weak she hadn't been able to resist. Not a single touch or caress; not even a single kiss! Leo had melted her into his arms and she had been able to do nothing, *nothing*, to hold back from him!

A shaft of fear went through her.

Three weeks, he'd said. Oh, God, she couldn't last three *days* here!

Or three nights…

She sat staring out over the beautiful vista of sea and sand as if she were staring at a desert of thorns.

He would do to her again tonight what he had done last night. She knew it. Knew it with a sick, dull certainty. He would take her to bed and stroke, caress and kiss her body until she could fight it no longer. Until her control was stripped from her just as he stripped the clothes from her body, and that mortal, consuming fire would ignite in her again—until she was aching for him…

Anna could feel her body start to respond, feel a prickling in her skin even at the memory of the night that had passed.

Agitatedly she got to her feet, crossing her arms over her chest, crushing down the sensation that was starting to lick at her body. The hunger that was coming to life again, the throb between her aching thighs…

She had to keep busy! Had to do something, anything, to distract her body. She'd already done her morning stretches and skincare routine, using them to blank out her mind as best she could, when she had finally stirred from her exhausted slumber to wake to lacerating consciousness. Sick with horror, she'd bolted from the bedroom, hearing the shower in the *en suite* bathroom, knowing she had to get away before he emerged.

Emerged to enjoy his triumph over her.

She'd stuck in her room, body aching, trembling with over-stimulation, wanting only to sink into permanent oblivion—anything other than face up to what she had done.

But there had been no oblivion—only a maid, insistent, not once but twice, that Mr Makarios was waiting for her on the terrace.

So she had put her armour on. Like one going into battle. Her exercise outfit was hardly the thing to wear in the Caribbean, but it was the only daywear she had brought with her that was not designed for the Alps in winter. She'd tied up her hair, put on the concealing veil of her dark glasses, and gone down to face up to what she had done.

Taking refuge from it the only way she knew how.

And she'd nearly cracked.

So very nearly.

As she'd walked up to him and seen him sitting there, lounging back, the strength of his body exposed in a close-hugging polo shirt, in hip-lean shorts, seen the long, strong sinews of his thighs, the smooth, muscled forearms, seen him watching her approach through lazy, heavy-lidded eyes, she had felt her insides start to dissolve.

He had just looked so devastating!

Something had turned over inside her, melting through her.

And then another emotion had taken its place. A familiar one—a safe one. The safest she could ever have in his company.

Anger.

That was what she had to feel in his presence—nothing but anger. It was the only way she could endure what lay ahead.

In the night, she knew, with bitter self-hatred, she would succumb—could do nothing else, was helpless to resist.

But in the day—

In the day the object of her hatred could be someone other than herself. It could be the man who had done to her the thing she could never, ever forgive herself for.

Leo Makarios—the man she both hated and desired.

CHAPTER SEVEN

Leo slewed the Jeep to a halt in front of the villa in the golden light of the westering sun. His muscles ached, but at least his black mood had gone. He'd spent the day on the island's eastern coast, punishing it out of him by wave-sailing the rough Atlantic swell. He'd thought of doing what he'd done yesterday—inspecting his property developments taking shape on the southern shores—but everything was going to schedule and there was nothing more there to occupy him. Besides, he hadn't come here to work. He'd come here to relax.

Unwind.

Enjoy some well-earned R&R with a beautiful woman to warm his bed...

His face darkened momentarily as he tossed the Jeep's keys at one of the outdoor staff and headed indoors. All day he'd deliberately kept Anna Delane out of his head. He didn't want to think about her.

Now he wondered idly how she'd spent the day. Still sulking?

A smile twisted at his mouth as he sprinted lithely upstairs. She wouldn't be sulking for long. He'd make sure of it.

There was no way a thieving piece like Anna Delane was going to get the better of him. His smile deepened.

He would start again on her, right now.

He'd just thought of an excellent way to do so.

A massage, personally administered, was exactly what he wanted.

And after the massage...

Anna lay in Leo Makarios's arms. She was facing away from him, drawn back against his body by his heavy, restraining arm. His thigh was heavy across hers.

She stared out across the room.

It had happened again.

The fire had burnt through her, burnt away every last vestige of her self-control, her self-respect.

A massage. She had been summoned to give him a massage. Like a slave girl!

She'd done it, too. Because what would have been the point of objecting? She'd been brought here for this purpose—the price of keeping her out of jail, keeping Jenny safe. And if a massage was what the man who thought her a thief wanted, then a massage was what he would have.

And what came after.

It had taken very, very little time for her kneading hands to be caught, stilled. For him to turn over with lithe, muscled grace onto his back, for him to draw her down on him again and then, with sudden avid hunger, to tip her over until he was over her. His mouth had been on hers, his hands on her body, peeling the clothes from her as if he were peeling a ripe, luscious fruit for his delectation.

And she had let him. Once more she had let him. Helpless to resist, helpless to do anything except let her body ignite from his, catch the hunger of his kisses, the ardency of his caressing.

Until she had burned with him in the same hot, fierce flame, crying out, her hair whipping, consumed absolutely by the sensation obliterating all sense from her, obliterating everything but its own desperate, urgent need for satiation.

Then afterwards, as the tumult had died, draining away like an inferno that had consumed its own fuel, he had lifted himself from her, rolling to his side, drawing her back against him, smoothing her hair, murmuring to her words she did not understand, his breath warm on her neck, his hands warm on her body.

And now she lay there, her body's conflagration slowly ebbing to its last cooling embers, exhausted, sated, feeling his chest rise and fall heavily behind her spine, knowing her lungs too were replenishing their air, her heart gradually slowing.

She lay staring out into the dusky room, hearing only the

susurration of his breathing, only the low hum of the air-conditioning.

Her mind seemed suspended, incapable of operation. She couldn't think, or feel, or make any conscious use of words or thoughts.

She seemed to be somewhere else.

Someone else.

And there was nothing, *nothing* she could do.

Leo lay, Anna enfolded in his arms. His body was warm, inert. So was hers. They were incapable of movement, both of them, he knew. The exhaustion that followed the little death had overtaken them both.

It felt good to hold her like this, spooned back against him.

It was as if she belonged to him.

His mind shifted. Where had that thought come from?

He did not want Anna Delane to belong to him. What would he want that for? She was a thief. A beautiful, desirable thief. But a thief for all that.

He did not want to get involved with her.

But then, he never wanted to get involved with any of the women he slept with. They kept to their own lives and he to his. He felt no desire for more.

Good sex was all he asked for, and a woman who knew not to make a nuisance of herself.

Let alone think she could steal a fortune from him with impunity.

Like the woman in his arms now.

He smoothed the hair back from her face a moment. Her eyes were open, but looking blankly ahead of her. He found himself wondering what she was thinking. What went on in her head?

He frowned. He *never* cared what went on in a woman's head. It was of no interest to him.

Was any other person of any interest to him? he found himself thinking.

His father had died of a heart attack seven years ago, and

his mother had moved to Melbourne to be with relatives. But he'd never been close to either of his parents. He'd seen little of his father while he was growing up, because his father, like his grandfather, had devoted his life to making the Makarios fortune. His mother had played her part by being a society hostess, assiduously cultivating anyone and everyone who could be useful to Makarios Corp. Which meant that her son had been handed over to nannies and teachers.

Possibly the closest person to him was Markos, with whom he'd shared some of his schooling, but now, as adults, they met up only sporadically. Both led the highly peripatetic lives of the very rich, each running their own separate portions of the vast Makarios corporation which inevitably took them in different physical directions much of the time.

He had an extensive staff, of course, ranging from key executives to a team of personal assistants. And he had friends. Of course he had friends. Every man in his position had friends. Usually far too damn many.

But were any of them close to him?

Was he interested in any of them other than for what use they were to Makarios Corp? None sprang to mind.

Impatiently, he put the thoughts from him. His life was good—very good. Makarios Corp was riding high, he was riding high. He was in the prime of life, fit and healthy, and he knew without false modesty that he'd been blessed with a physical appearance that would be enviable even in a poor man. Combine that with his riches and he was a man other men envied and women wanted.

Anna Delane didn't...

The words stole into his head before he could stop them.

Anna Delane didn't want you—she threw you from her bedroom. Screeched her head off at you. Rejected you royally!

Deliberately he made himself stroke her arm, slowly, possessively. She wasn't rejecting him now—but the choice had been between him or jail...no wonder she hadn't rejected him! he thought bitterly.

Leo's jaw tightened.

Anna Delane would not have gone on rejecting him. He'd have seen to that. If he hadn't caught her red-handed with the Levantsky bracelet he'd still have pursued her. Whatever hypocritical reason she'd had for rejecting him that evening, he'd have got her in the end. Women didn't hold out on him. His usual problem was quite the opposite—fending them off. No, he'd have got Anna Delane in his bed. Thief or no.

It was a pity she was a thief...

Again, the words stole into his brain before he could stop them. They annoyed him. Obviously he'd have preferred her not to be a thief—after all, she'd come far too damn close to walking off with the Levantsky bracelet!—but that was the only reason for his preference. It would have made no other difference. The end result would have been the same. Her in his bed, a few weeks together, and then he'd tire of her.

His hand moved slowly up her arm again, enjoying her soft, silken skin.

He felt his body begin to stir.

No chance of tiring of her yet.

He shifted his weight onto his elbow, and cupped her chin, turning her head towards him. His mouth lowered to hers.

It felt good. Arousing.

Yes, definitely no chance of tiring of her yet.

Carefully, Anna smoothed total sunblock over her legs. Even though she spent as much time as she could in the shade, and put sunblock on religiously, she still seemed to be browning. She frowned. It was a damned nuisance. Her white skin was one of her selling points, and she guarded it assiduously. OK, so she could have stayed indoors every day, but she couldn't bear to. It was bad enough just getting through the days, without being denied the run of the gardens and the beach. Or the pool.

Thank God for the pool. Swimming up and down occupied hours of her time, and a swimsuit was something she never travelled without. Although she had enough evening outfits—brought for her time at the Schloss—daywear suitable for the

Caribbean climate was more of a problem. By dint of washing her exercise outfit daily, and wearing the jade-green silk trouser suit during the day, she was just managing to cope. She could also, during the day, wander round with just a towel wrapped round her like a sarong. That was because—and she thanked all the gods there were—Leo Makarios was never around in the daytime.

Maybe he sleeps in his earth-filled coffin in daytime? she thought acidly.

The reality, she knew, was more prosaic. He took himself off on the water. He seemed, thankfully, to have a whole range of ways of enjoying himself out at sea. Sometimes she saw him on a windsurf board, racing across the bay in a crosswind; sometimes—according to her cautious enquires of the house staff—he went to the Atlantic coast for stronger winds and wave-sailing and kite-surfing. Often he disappeared off in a variety of sailing craft. He seemed to have a whole collection in a boathouse further along the beach. She saw him skimming along in a one-handed dinghy, or on windier days taking a catamaran out, spinnaker billowing. He went off diving, too, some days, and she watched the staff lug oxygen tanks on board the inflatable dive boat, then him heading out to the reefs.

Whatever took him out to sea, she was just grateful.

It gave her precious respite time—without which, she knew, she would have cracked.

How many days had passed since she'd been brought here? She was losing count. It was coming up to two weeks, it must be. Or was it longer? She had tried not to count, tried not to think. The moon was changing, at its peak now, sailing serene and high far above the ocean, mocking her with its romantic beauty.

But then the whole place mocked her.

It could have been a paradise on earth. Instead it was her prison. Her place of torment.

A place where Leo Makarios tormented her to the utmost of his malign powers.

Night after night she burnt like a flame in his arms as he wrung from her the response he would not let her rest without.

The response she could not let herself rest without..

He had become a poison for her. A poison that had got into her bloodstream and which she was now utterly, completely dependent on.

And the poison was desire.

Abject, helpless desire.

It mortified her, humiliated her, lacerated her.

But it held her in its thrall.

And she knew she could not free herself from it now—she had succumbed to it abjectly, helplessly. Succumbed to Leo Makarios and what he could make her feel.

Every day when he came back to the villa her heart gave a leap. She tried to crush it, but it would not be crushed. She felt her breath quicken in her lungs, felt a rush of pleasure. Of anticipation.

Sometimes he took her to his bed immediately. Walking up to her, catching her hand, and taking her upstairs. She would feel her body quickening even as she went with him, feel the warm, delicious flood of arousal start in her body. She was as ardent as he; she could not help it. She wanted to feel his mouth on hers, his hands on her body, her hands on his, their bodies seeking, melding, fusing together in a rush of desire so intense it consumed her, time, after time, after time.

It had been a revelation—never had she understood how raw, how powerful, desire could be. Leo Makarios had taken her to a new place, one she had not known existed.

It was a place of passion, of ecstasy, of wanting and needing, of sating and slaking.

She knew no peace. Not during the day, when her restless body waited in forced patience for his return. Not when he was there either, and she went to him and let him take her in that white rush of desire as she took him into her. No peace then, only hunger, a driving, pulsing hunger that was a desperate, ravening need for what he and he alone could give her.

She knew only the brief, strange peace that came after, when their bodies were spent and they lay, exhausted, in each other's arms.

As if they were lovers.

But they weren't lovers. She knew that. Knew it deep in her being. There was nothing between them. Neither knowledge nor intimacy.

They were strangers. Day after day. Night after night.

Nothing but strangers.

A dull, crushing heaviness filled her as she sat, now, putting cream on her legs, before plunging into the warm waters of the pool. She looked around. There was a house full of staff tending the villa and its grounds—other human beings who lived and breathed and had hopes and ambitions and families and friends and loved ones—and yet she was all on her own.

You're always on your own. You always have been.

The thought distilled in her mind. It was true. It had always been true. Her grandmother loved her dearly, had brought her up single-handed after her mother's death, with her father long since disappeared into whatever wasteland involuntary fathers disappeared to. But her grandmother, for all her love, all her protection, was two generations away from her—happy with her little world in the street of terraced houses beside the gasworks, happy to spend the day watching soaps and chat shows, and scared to let Anna go out into the world. Let alone take up modelling.

Her grandmother hated it; she'd always known that. Warning her about the evils of the life she was heading for. But she could not have turned down her one big chance to get away from the gasworks and the beckoning biscuit factory. She'd always visited her grandmother as often as she could, and the years had passed, and she'd become too infirm in body and mind to go on living in her little terraced house. Now she passed her time in an expensive private nursing home, paid for by her granddaughter's modelling fees, sometimes recognising her when she visited, sometimes not.

Who will I have when my grandmother dies? Who will I have then?

The question echoed in her head as she stared out over the azure sea beyond.

She had some friends—good friends like Jenny, with whom she'd bonded in the frenetic, superficial, all too often corrupt and corrupting world of fashion modelling, and a few others that she trusted. But, valuable as her friends were, they each had someone special in their lives. Even Jenny had the child she would bear, in secrecy and safety, in her new life that she would make for herself in Australia.

I could go with her.

The thought came from nowhere.

And even as it formed a terrible heaviness came in its wake.

When Leo Makarios is finished with me—what shall I do?

She had thought she would simply go back to her life. Had thought nothing else.

But now, with punishing clarity, she knew it was impossible, that her life was empty.

She could never go back.

Her life as a model seemed a million miles away from here. On another planet.

She could never go back to it.

And the terrible heaviness crushed at her. She would have to leave here. One day, coming closer day by day, when Leo was bored with her, when he'd decided she'd made reparation enough, when some business crisis cropped up, needing his attention in New York, or Geneva, or London, then he would simply go.

And she would be bundled onto a plane and disposed of.

She would never see him again.

Never.

The word clanged in her head like a stone.

A bitter mockery filled her. Dear God. Once, brief days ago, if someone had said she would never see Leo Makarios again she'd have felt a relief so profound it would have lifted her off the ground.

Now—now it tolled like a funeral bell. Filling her with dread.

And there was an ache in her body that she could not extinguish.

An anguish.

An anguish that filled her being.

She stared out over the silver sand, the azure waters. Paradise on earth.

But, for her, the worst place in the world.

A place of unimaginable, exquisite torment.

Leo limped, bad tempered, out onto the terrace, and looked down across to the pool deck. Anna was swimming up and down with her graceful stroke. He watched her a while. It was strange seeing her during the daytime. Deliberately, he never let himself think about her when he was away from the villa. He just put her out of his mind, focusing instead on things like making a fast tack in the cat, or doing some tricky freestyle move on his board. He glowered. The damn loop he'd been working on yesterday had caught him out—and down he'd gone into the water, foot still caught in the footstrap. The result was a badly wrenched ankle. At least it wasn't a break or a sprain—the doctor had confirmed it just now. But he'd also stipulated resting his foot. No more watersports for a few days.

So what the hell was he going to do all day now? He'd deliberately kept his work to a minimum—an hour morning and evening, communicating remotely with his direct reports and a handful of key people, was all he allowed himself. He didn't want to get sucked back in.

He stood, watching Anna swim up and down. Well, he could swim too—just about. Moodily, he headed down, tossing his dark glasses on a chair. He limped to the deep end and dived in.

He powered down the length, making his turn with one foot only, pushing off, and powering down to the deep end. Over and over—ten, twenty, thirty, forty lengths. Working off something he needed to work off.

As he finally touched the wall at the end of his fortieth length and stood up, shaking the water from his hair, he saw Anna was still in the pool, doggedly breaststroking up and down her side, taking no notice of him as usual.

A familiar stab of irritation went through Leo. The damn girl totally ignored his existence whenever she could. She answered him tersely, her reluctance visible, whenever he tried to talk to her. He'd got to the point where he damned her as much as she was clearly damming him. Hell, he hadn't brought her here for conversation, but for sex—and that she definitely didn't stint him.

Leo stood in the water, leaning back against the stone surround, crooked arms resting on the tiles around the pool. He felt his mood improve. No, Anna Delane certainly didn't stint him on the sex front.

In bed now she definitely, definitely purred.

A slow smile parted his lips. He'd achieved what he'd intended—to have Anna Delane panting for him, hungry for him. No more virtuous outrage when he dared to lay a caressing hand on her. No, now she trembled with her need for him the moment he touched her. He only had to look at her and see the desire flare in her eyes, the hunger...

A sense of satisfaction went through him. Anna Delane purred for him in bed—and now, since he could not go out on the sea, he would amuse himself getting her to purr for him out of bed. It would, he decided, be a personal challenge.

He'd take her shopping. The island had some upmarket designer outlets, and shopping always put women in a good mood. Especially when some man was picking up the tab.

Besides, a woman like Anna Delane was used to the fast life—sophisticated cities and endless parties. Being deprived of them was probably contributing to her sulkiness.

An idea came to him. He'd take her shopping today, and then tomorrow he'd start socialising with her. There was a whole bunch of people on the island—from useful local business and government contacts to wealthy European ex-pats, either living or wintering here—who would always welcome him as a guest. He'd put in a few calls—let people know he was here.

I'll show Anna off to them...

The thought came from nowhere and stopped him in his tracks.

A frown creased his brow. Show Anna Delane off to his friends? Show off a thief? A woman who was earning her freedom from jail in his bed?

No, she wasn't a woman to show off. She was a woman to keep secret, private. Hidden for his own pleasure.

As if he were ashamed of her...

Of himself...

Something stabbed through him. It did not feel comfortable.

Leo shook it away. He did not like to feel uncomfortable about himself.

With a rasp of irritation he levered himself out of the pool. His damaged ankle told him he'd probably swum too vigorously, so a day taking it easy was definitely a good idea. He limped to the other side of the pool and waited until Anna had finished her length.

To his annoyance, even though he was crouched down just where her length ended, clearly intending to speak to her, she still didn't register his presence. She was all set to do a breaststroke turn. His hand shot out, closing around her forearm as she seized the end of the pool with both hands, ready to plunge round.

She stopped abruptly.

'I haven't finished my lengths,' she told him coldly.

'You've done enough,' he told her. 'Up you come.'

His hand closed over her other forearm. Pinioned, Anna glowered at him, then let him pull her out of the pool in a strong, lithe movement. She stood, water dripping off her, hair slicked back in a high ponytail.

'Yes?' she said, just as coldly.

'Get dried and changed,' he told her, limping across to where her towel was draped on another pool chair and helping himself to it. 'We're going out.'

'What?'

He looked at her, dripping and stiff-bodied, as he patted his chest with her towel.

'I said, we're going out.'

'I don't want to go out,' she riposted instantly.

Her attitude annoyed him—as it always did.

'But I do,' he replied. 'And I want you to come with me.'

She just went on staring at him.

'What for? '

'Indulge me,' he returned sardonically.

A slight flush of colour flared over her cheekbones. Then her face tightened.

'I thought I only had to do that in bed!' she snapped.

Something equivalent snapped in Leo. Hell, the girl was hard work. And right now he was in no mood to put up with it.

'*Thee mou*, I simply want to go out for the day. What's the big deal? Lighten up, Anna—you might even enjoy it. After all…' his voice changed, and the sardonic note was back in it, taunting her '…you've come round to enjoying the rest of what I give you, haven't you.'

This time the colour definitely flared out across her cheekbones. For a moment Leo mistook it for embarrassment. Then he realised it must just be temper. Well, Anna Delane could be as cussed as she liked—and, *Christos*, did she like!—but he wanted to go out, and he wanted her to come with him. And what he wanted, he got.

He always did.

He limped off, and Anna watched him go, glowering.

What the hell was going on? she fumed. She didn't want to go anywhere with Leo Makarios. And why was he wanting to take her anywhere anyway? Why wasn't he going off in one of his boats or whatever? She watched him head across the terrace. Was he limping? Yes, he was. Quite badly.

A sudden pang darted through her. For a moment—quite insanely—she wanted to go after him and express concern. Ask him what he'd done to his foot.

She crushed it down. Leo Makarios could go under a train for all she cared…

Liar...

Emotion twisted in her. She tried to crush that down too, but it would not be banished. Despairingly she shut her eyes.

I can't face a day out with him—I just can't!

It was taking all her strength to cope with the nights, to cope with the terrible, treacherous reaction of her body to his touch. She could cope only because she kept the night to the night, and at all other times either minimised her time in his company or shut him out as much as she could.

But now she was going to have to spend a whole day in his company.

Heaviness pressed on her.

She opened her eyes again. Leo had disappeared inside the house.

With a weariness of spirit she did not want to think about, she followed him.

Anna stared about her. Not only did it make it easier to ignore the man driving the four-by-four careering along the potted road, but it was interesting to see something more of the island than the Makarios villa—exquisite though that was.

From the air-conditioned interior the rolling landscape looked lush, covered in wild greenery. Little villages were dotted about, the West Indian chattel-style board houses surrounded by banana trees and their verandas over-tumbled with crimson bougainvillaea. Roadside stalls every now and then sold fresh fruit, both to islanders and to tourists stopping off in their hire cars to taste fresh pineapple and coconut.

She didn't ask where they were going—what was the point? She would find out when they got there. But when they did, Anna was surprised. It was the capital of the island, and Leo made his way, weaving along a grid of streets, to end up by the harbour. He parked the car and nodded at Anna.

'Time to go shopping,' he announced.

He waited for her expression to brighten at the treat ahead, but she simply kept the same blank expression on her face that

she always kept for him. Pressing his mouth tightly, he got ou
and waited while she did likewise.

The mid-morning heat hit her, and she instantly felt the in
appropriateness of the tight-fitting stretch clothes she was wear
ing. Had he really said shopping? Well, thank heavens for that
at least. At last she could buy some beachwear.

So it was with more enthusiasm than Leo usually saw in her
outside the bedroom that she followed him into the smartest
looking tax-free designer wear shop. Swiftly and methodically
she sifted along the rails and took her selection to the cash
desk.

Leo was there before her.

'So at last you've seen sense enough to wear something suit
able for the beach,' he said pointedly, indicating her armful o
brightly coloured clothes.

She stared at him tightly.

'Strangely,' she informed him acidly, 'I wasn't planning
trip to the Caribbean when I packed for Austria. Of course
didn't have any suitable daywear for the beach!'

Leo frowned. 'You mean you've been wearing those idioti
outfits because it was all you had? Good grief, why didn't you
just tell me? I could have taken you shopping the day you
arrived!' He spoke as if she were stupid.

Anna said nothing, merely smiled at the saleslady and let
her start folding her clothes.

'You don't want to try any on?' asked Leo sceptically.

She cast him a look. 'I can tell they'll fit, and I can tell
they'll suit me. It's one of the little skills you pick up in my
line of work.'

'There is no call for sarcasm,' Leo replied repressively
'When I take women shopping they usually spend hours trying
on everything in sight. It's a dead bore. Your attitude is re
freshing, believe me.'

He started reaching inside his back trouser pocket for his
wallet. But Anna was already handing her credit card over.

'Anna,' he said, even more repressively, 'allow me, if you
please.'

'I don't please,' she said, and nodded at the saleslady to take her card.

Leo sighed heavily. 'Are you trying to prove something, Anna?'

'No. I'm just buying my own clothes.'

With a snap, Leo put his wallet away. Let the damn girl buy her own clothes if she insisted. He watched her sign for her purchases, pick up the bags, and then hesitate suddenly.

'I'd like to change,' she said to the shop assistant, and disappeared with the bags.

She emerged in under two minutes, clad in a brightly coloured blue and orange sundress that floated around her calves.

Leo found his breath stilling. She really was the most stunning female he'd laid eyes on. Effortlessly so. Her hair was still in its high ponytail, and she'd let it dry naturally, without any styling. She wore no make-up except suncream and protective lipgloss. And sunshades. Not a scrap of jewellery either.

And yet in that simple print dress she looked breathtaking.

Something moved inside him. It was an odd sensation. He didn't know what it was.

He only knew it was inappropriate.

'Let's go,' he said shortly, and headed outdoors.

Anna followed him, feeling the relief of finally wearing something that didn't look idiotic in these tropical surroundings.

'There's another designer shop over there.' Leo pointed across the way and started towards it.

'I've got all the clothes I need,' Anna returned.

Leo gave a snort. 'No woman has all the clothes she needs! And this time—' he turned his head '—I am buying. Please do not make another scene.'

Anna's lips tightened.

'I really don't want any more clothes,' she insisted.

'Then what do you want?' He glanced around, eyes lighting on a jewellery store. For a moment he realised he was on the point of buying her jewels, as if she were an ordinary mistress.

Anna couldn't help but see where he'd been looking.

'No, thank you,' she said sweetly. 'I prefer to steal mine.'

Leo's head whipped round, eyes narrowed.

His eyes fastened on hers.

And for a second—quite inexplicably—he suddenly wanted to laugh. The girl was outrageous, all right! Totally outrageous—and yet...

He broke eye contact deliberately, pointing out a souvenir shop selling island art and mementoes.

Anna shook her head sharply.

'I'll have all the souvenirs of this place I could never want,' she said.

Leo's eyes slashed back to hers. This time he didn't want to laugh at all. He wanted to throttle her.

'Well, your souvenirs from an Austrian jail would be very different, I can assure you!' he shot back tightly. He took her arm. 'I need some coffee,' he announced.

She tried to pull away from him, but he would not let her.

'Let go of me!' she snarled.

He merely tightened his grip, and looked down at her with his long-lashed eyes.

'That's not what you say in bed, Anna *mou*. You want me to touch you then.'

His voice was soft, as soft as silk, his eyes molten, melting her...

Once again he saw colour flare out along her cheekbones, and that look in her eyes. Of all things, it looked as if it was embarrassment. But that was impossible. Anna Delane was a thief, shameless and unapologetic, and the life she lived as a fashion model hardly meant she was embarrassable about sex.

Then he saw her chin go up, her mouth tighten, as if she were suppressing something. Her body was as stiff as a board.

'I thought you said you wanted a coffee,' she bit at him.

CHAPTER EIGHT

ANNA sat at the little harbourside café, watching the boats at their mooring. This was no flash marina—most of the boats were working boats: ferries to other islands, or freighters, or fishing boats.

Opposite her, Leo sat and glowered.

Anna was ignoring him—as usual. Looking at anything and everything except him. Sipping black coffee with a stony face. Exasperation swept through him again. She looked a million dollars in that sundress, and yet she'd insisted on buying it herself—and the others in the bags around her feet. Her insistence infuriated him, and he was annoyed at himself for feeling so unreasonably ill-tempered about it. What the hell was she up to, refusing to let him buy her those paltry clothes?

As if she were making some kind of point to him.

But what kind of point was Anna Delane entitled to make to him? None, that was what. Yet she was as prickly as a hedgehog, trying to make *him* feel bad when it was *she* who was the criminal. Leo's teeth clenched. Why the hell couldn't she just be *nice* for once? Pleasant, attentive, eager to please? Eager, if nothing else, to earn the parole he'd promised her?

But not her. No. No, she was sitting there, ignoring him, chin in the air as if she had a bad smell underneath her fastidious nose.

From the corner of her averted eye, Anna saw Leo glowering at her. She refused to look at him. Every instinct told her not to.

Yet something was pulling at her. Something that made her want to just tilt her head slightly, so very, very slightly. Just a little. Just enough to see more of Leo Makarios than from the corner of her eye. To see him sitting there, lounging back in

125

his chair, long legs extended, lean, taut body displayed for her dark, molten eyes pouring through her, melting her...

No!

Doggedly she held her head rigid. Refusing to look at him. It seemed suddenly essential that she did not look at him.

She lifted her coffee cup one last time, and set it down empty. And as she did so, of their own volition, pulled by something she could not prevent, her eyes were drawn to him

To feast on him like a starving man.

Yes! Leo all but punched the air. He'd got her. Her eyes had wandered to him—wandered, and stuck. With absolute self-control he reached for his coffee, holding his gaze impassive. He lifted his cup, relaxing back in his seat, stretching out his legs and flexing his shoulders. He could see her expression register the movement, and his mood improved yet again. He sat back, letting her gaze at him, his own glowering expression quite vanished now.

He luxuriated in her covert observation for a few moments longer, then said, 'Where would you like to go next, Anna?'

Immediately, her gaze cut out. The look of deliberate indifference was back in her face.

'I have no opinion on the subject,' she replied, and pretended to drink more coffee.

'Then I'll choose, shall I?' said Leo, with exaggerated politeness.

'Please do.' She gave her acid-sweet smile again.

And again, for one bizarre moment, as his eyes caught hers, Leo wanted to laugh out loud. The girl was impossible, outrageous, infuriating—yet there was something about Anna Delane that he could not let go of...

Leo got to his feet, tossing some East Caribbean dollars down on the table. Incredulously, he watched Anna open her purse, then pause.

'I don't have any local currency,' she announced. She glanced around and saw a bank on the corner of one of the streets leading back into the town. Without pausing, she darted across and went in. She emerged a few minutes later and came back to their table, putting down some coins next to his notes.

'Take them back, Anna,' Leo said, in a low, dangerous voice.

His good mood had gone—totally. He was right back to wanting to throttle her.

She stared at him. 'I'm paying,' she said, 'for my coffee.'

Greek issued from him in a staccato fire. 'God almighty, is this some kind of joke?' He caught her wrist, halting her. 'You stole a bracelet from me worth at a conservative estimate eighty thousand euros. Don't even *think* of trying to make yourself look virtuous by paying for your own damn coffee and clothes.' He brought his face closer to hers. 'You're a thief—nothing but a thief. Don't ever think I am going to forget that and be impressed by you.'

Anna's face had gone rigid. Her eyes were like pinpricks of green fire.

'Understand this, and understand it well, Leo Makarios,' she hissed at him. 'I wouldn't stoop to trying to impress you if it was my last day on earth. Think what you want of me—I don't give a stuff!'

She twisted out of his grip, and stormed off.

Leo stared after her fulminatingly, then set off after her.

Damn the girl. Damn her to hell! She should be begging him to go easy on her! Should be using all her arts and beauty to try and captivate him, soothe his savage heart and plead for a lighter sentence. She should be making up to him, eager for his approval, his attention.

The way other women did.

Other women always made up to him, sought his attention, his interest. They put themselves out for him, exerting all their charms. They wanted to please him.

And yet Anna Delane, who had stolen *his* rubies and never shown the slightest sign of contrition about it, who had a thousand, million times more cause to want to please him, was as eager to please him as a piranha was to be a vegetarian!

She's different in bed. In bed she wants everything you give her...

His eyes shadowed. Yes, but even there, he realised, eager as she was to take the pleasure he bestowed on her, she never, unless he instructed her, took any initiative sexually. Oh, she did as he bade her, and enjoyed it too, he knew that—taking sensual pleasure in caressing him, arousing him, sating him.

But she never did it spontaneously. Never to please him because she wanted to please him. Because she wanted him to be pleased with her. Indulgent of her.

The way other women did.

He thought of Delia Delatore, his last mistress, and the French countess who had been her predecessor. He thought of the parade of women who had passed through his bed.

Every single one of them had always wanted to please him. Because each and every one of them had known how fortunate they were for having been chosen by him. They had known how lucky they were that his eyes had lighted on them and selected them for his bed.

All except one.

Memory stung in his brain like acid.

Anna Delane—on whom he had looked with desire, with wanting, and to whose bedroom he had come, expecting exactly the same reception as every other woman had given him.

And she'd thrown him out on his ear.

Rejected him and scorned him and berated him.

Anger and chagrin pulsed through him.

Then another thought occurred.

Yes, but she was planning all along to steal the rubies.

But that should have made her even more eager to lull him into a sense of false security with her. He'd have been far less likely to suspect her if she'd been pleasing him in bed—for a start, her motivation would have been a lot less. The bracelet might be worth eighty thousand euros, but that was on the open market. Anna Delane would have had to fence it, and whatever she made out of the sale it wouldn't have been eighty thousand.

Yet as his mistress, pleasing him sufficiently to be kept for several weeks, she must have known she would easily have walked away with gifts of jewellery worth much more than her profit from stealing the Levantsky jewels.

And so much less risky...

So why, *why* had she thrown him out of her bedroom like that?

It simply didn't make sense.

He strode after her, to where she was waiting by the car. She looked like a cat who'd had its fur rubbed up the wrong way. He could almost see her tail lashing furiously.

He unlocked the door and she climbed in, whisking her skirts gracefully inside as she sat. She belted herself up, then stared rigidly ahead out of the window.

He wondered whether her teeth were gritted. He wouldn't be surprised. He could feel his own gritting.

A thought darted into his head.

Why do we keep fighting?

It came from nowhere, and he amended it immediately— *Why does she keep fighting me?* But it didn't work. The original version was the one that bit at him as he headed out of town.

There is no 'we'. There can be no possibility of there being a 'we'.

He put his good foot down, and shot off.

Perhaps a decent lunch would make him feel better.

Anna looked around her. They'd driven for over forty-five minutes across the interior of the island. She'd spent her time as before, gazing around at the landscape and the scenery. Now they were driving along a twisting narrow lane, slowing every now and then as goats wandered, grazing at the roadside. One final twist, and a stone gateway was opening to their left. Leo swung the car through, into a paved area dotted with cars. He pulled into a parking space and cut the engine.

'Where are we?'

Anna stared around, not looking at Leo as she asked her question.

Amazing, thought Leo caustically. She's asked a question. Graciously, he supplied an answer.

'It's an old plantation house that's been converted into a restaurant.' He leant across to open her door, ignoring the way her body automatically stiffened and pulled away, as if to avoid him.

'Shall we?' he enquired, even more graciously.

He drew back his hand and Anna undid her seat belt, breathing out again. She climbed down, feeling the noon-day heat of the Caribbean hit her. She flexed her shoulders and looked around her.

'This way,' said Leo, at her side.

She walked along beside him, doing her best to ignore him, but highly conscious of his presence. But then, she always was conscious of his presence, she thought wearily.

Why can't I be immune to him? Why can't he just be like a block of wood?

She gave a sigh. It didn't help to ask such hopeless questions. Leo Makarios had an effect on her that she could not ignore. Even though she desperately longed to.

How much longer can I endure this? How much more can I take? Wanting him and hating him, and hating myself for wanting him, and...

The questions drummed in her head like a pain in her skull. Numbly she followed the stone-paved pathway that led upwards through tropical gardens. The heat settled on her shoulders, making her feel heavy and tired.

She paused, suppressing another sigh.

'Are you all right?'

Her head twisted in surprise.

'What?'

Leo's eyes flashed briefly.

'Are you feeling all right?' he repeated.

'I'm fine,' she answered shortly, and made to go on walking.

A hand stayed her, cupping around her bare elbow. She wanted to pull away, but there was something about his grip that held her.

'What?' she demanded, this time resisting the impulse to look at him.

'Anna—listen to me.'

There was something different about his voice. She didn't know what it was, but it made her look at him. His face was sombre. The expression quite different from any she had seen. For a moment she just looked at him, a slight puzzle in her eyes.

'Stop—fighting—me.'

The words came heavily, the look he levelled at her even heavier.

A lump seemed to be forming in her throat. It made it difficult for her to speak, but she forced herself. Her chin went up, jaw tightening.

'Tell me something,' she shot back. 'Why do you care less if I fight you or not? Why do you care about anything except getting what you want in bed?' There was a challenge in her voice. A bitter defiance.

Something shadowed his eyes, so briefly she thought she must have imagined it. Then he answered her.

'Because I'm tired, Anna. I'm tired and fed up, and my ankle hurts, and I'm hungry, and you've given me nothing but grief, and I just want—I just want an easy day for once. OK? Is that so big a deal? Can we really not just this once have a civil, civilised meal together, without you giving me the big freeze the whole damn time?'

Anna's eyes narrowed to slits. 'Why *should* I? Tell me that. You get the night times! The rest of the day you can go whistle!'

She saw his jaw clench, then slowly unclench.

'I'll do a deal with you. A one-off special. Just while my ankle is bad. Tonight you can have off, if—*if* you lose the attitude today.'

Anna looked at him. Was he serious? Or was this just another baiting mockery of her?

'Do you mean it?' she demanded.

'Oh, yes. Tonight, providing you behave like a normal

woman today, you can sleep in your own bed. If, of course—'
and suddenly the baiting, mocking look she'd been expecting
was there '—you want to.'

Her green eyes flashed. 'Oh, I want to all right.'

His dark eyes glinted. She thought it was anger, but was not
sure. 'Then we have a deal?' he posed.

For one moment longer she went on glaring at him. Then
she gave a brief nod. After all, she had no choice, did she? Leo
Makarios was blackmailing her into sex—any chance she got
to escape a night of 'reparation' had to be grabbed—didn't it?

*Of course it does! Grab it with both hands! Because if you
don't you'll know—and he'll know—why you don't! And your
humiliation at his hands will be complete. Your defeat total.*

The thought was unbearable. Only one thing in the world
would be worse than Leo Makarios knowing how weak, how
vulnerable she was to him.

And that would be him knowing it as well. She would endure
anything to prevent that. Even endure having a civil lunch with
him.

He let go her elbow.

'Good,' was all he said.

He set off along the path again, leaving her to follow.

Lunch was served at tables set out under a wide awning on a
terrace with a breathtaking view down over the bay below. A
cooling breeze wafted gently, making the heat comfortable.

Anna took her place, gazing out over the vista. It really was
beautiful, she thought, and for a moment a pang struck her so
deep that it was like the thrust of a knife.

*It's so idyllic, so magical! Why can't I be here with someone
else? Why does it have to be Leo Makarios?*

But even as the words formed she knew they were not true.
The knife twisted painfully.

*It's not because it's Leo Makarios—it's because of the rea-
son I'm here with him. That's what's so awful!*

Her eyes looked out over the vivid greens of the vegetation, the brilliant azure of the sea, and she felt an ache start inside her—a longing so great that she felt overwhelmed by it.

Oh, God, if only he didn't think me a thief! If he didn't think me a thief I could be—

Another voice cut across her mind. Harsh and punishing.

You could be what? His mistress? His sex toy while he wants you, and then dumped for the next one that takes his eye?

Her eyes hardened. Yes, that was the best she could ever be for Leo Makarios. A man who regarded women as mistresses. To be enjoyed, pampered and then disposed of. Hadn't she heard the way he spoke about Vanessa and his cousin Markos? Why should she assume Leo would think any better of *her*, even if he didn't believe she was a thief?

Heavily, she picked up the menu lying in front of her.

'Anna—' Leo's voice was a warning. She flicked her eyes to him questioningly.

'Yes?' she responded brusquely.

There was a frown in his eyes.

'We have a deal, remember?'

For a moment his eyes held hers, and for a moment she looked back at him with her usual baleful expression.

'Give it a rest, Anna,' he said wearily.

She slapped her menu down. 'How can I?' she breathed vehemently. 'You want me to suck up to you, don't you? Like the rest of your women! Fawn all over you and pander to you and—'

'No.' The negation snapped from him.

Anna's eyes flashed.

'Yes, you do. That's your idea of normality from a woman. You can't cope with a woman treating you without kid gloves.'

A look of annoyance darkened his face.

'You are being ridiculous,' he replied brusquely. 'I require only that my partner is...' he shrugged, clearly searching for a word, then found it '...gracious,' he concluded. 'And why,' he went on swiftly, 'would she wish to be otherwise?'

There was an arrogant question in his expression that exasperated Anna even more, because it showed her exactly what his problem was. Then, with a silent sigh, she subsided. Leo Makarios was rich and gorgeous—no wonder he was spoilt by women. No wonder they sucked up to him, fawning over him, craving him...

Her mind snapped shut. No. She must not think about craving Leo Makarios...desiring him...wanting him so much that night after night she melted her body against his, putting aside, forgetting deliberately, in that burning inferno that consumed her, that the only reason she was in his bed was because the grim alternative was prison...

But I'm in prison anyway—a prison I can never escape from...a prison of passion, of desire, that cages me in night after night...

Except that tonight, if she accepted Leo's temporary bargain, she would have parole from that prison.

If she could bring herself to be 'civil' to the man who was reducing her to such abjectness.

Her chin lifted. She could—she must. For one night at least she might have a reprieve from the prison she went to so helplessly, night after night.

Her eyes went back to the menu, leaving unanswered Leo's arrogant challenge. For a moment longer she felt his gaze resting on her, as if waiting for her to throw yet another pointless dart at his colossal ego, then she felt him relax. So, minutely, did she, and fell to perusing the range of delicious options— none of which, as ever, she had any intention of choosing.

Yet even as she was mentally closing the menu, prepared to content herself with grilled fish and undressed salad, so, out of nowhere, a spark of rebellion ignited. If she was to get through the day being 'civil' to Leo Makarios, then at least she could have some compensation for her ordeal.

When the waiter came to enquire if they were ready to order, on impulse she lifted her head, closed the menu, and announced that she would have prawns fried in coconut milk, served with rice. And she would drink wine as well.

And calories be hanged! After all, she had something to celebrate—a night off from Leo Makarios.

Without volition, her eyes strayed to him as he finished giving the waiter his own order, and then accepted the wine menu from the hovering sommelier. He was studying the list, brows drawn in faint concentration. She felt emotion pour through her. She waited for it to be anger. That was the safe emotion to feel about Leo Makarios.

The only safe one.

But it wasn't anger. Instead, a different emotion seemed to be taking her over. One she had no business feeling—none at all. None. But she felt it all the same.

She went on gazing at him, drinking him in.

I could look at him all day...

All night....

For ever.

Cold chilled through her as the words formed unbidden in her head. She tried to push them away, undo them, unthink them. She must not let them be said, thought.

Deliberately, she forced herself to keep staring at him.

The dark hair, the planes of his face, those potent heavy-lidded eyes, the wide, sensual mouth, the hard line of his jaw—all were achingly familiar. There wasn't an inch of his face, his body, that she had not kissed, caressed, touched.

But it's the face of a stranger. A complete stranger.

A stranger who can never, never be anything else.

For a moment so brief, and yet so agonising, she sat there, surrounded by other couples, other families, chatting away, eating and drinking in this beautiful place, shaded from the hot sun, yet basking in its balmy warmth, with the deep blue bay and emerald green coastline sweeping before them, and wished, suddenly, deeply, out of nowhere, that she and Leo Makarios were just one of those couples.

Any of them—young or old, good-looking or plain—it didn't matter. But to be here like them, on holiday, together...a real couple...

Not his blackmailed bed partner, not his pampered mistress—but something far, far more to him...

Angrily, she smashed the image to pieces in her mind. She

was insane even to think such a thing about Leo Makarios. Her expression tightened and she picked up her glass, sipping sparkling mineral water, making herself look back over the vista beyond. She saw from the corner of her eye Leo give his choice to the sommelier, who then glided away.

She felt a hand tug at her skirt and looked round—then down.

A small moppet of a child was standing beside her, holding up her wrist.

'I've got a new bracelet,' she informed Anna.

Her eyes were blue, her hair curly, her sundress pink. So was the bracelet, of pink polished coral.

'So you have,' agreed Anna with a smile. 'It's very pretty.'

'My mummy bought it for me from a lady on the beach,' the moppet said.

'Lucy!' A woman's voice called from a nearby table. 'Don't bother the lady, darling.'

Anna looked across to where an Englishwoman in her thirties was lunching with her husband and a little boy.

'She's not bothering me at all,' she reassured the woman. 'I'm admiring her beautiful bracelet.'

The woman laughed. 'She's showing it off to everyone she can.'

Anna smiled. 'Why not? It's lovely.' She looked down at the little girl again. Her smile deepened. 'It's a *very* pretty bracelet,' she told the child again.

The little girl nodded, satisfied with this response, and moved off to the next table to repeat the exercise with the woman there. Her mother got up and gently guided her back to their own table.

'Your ice-cream will be here any moment, Lucy—come along.'

She cast a conspiratorial smile at Anna as her daughter, duly diverted, scurried back to her place.

Anna smiled back, but noticed how the woman's eyes had automatically strayed towards Leo. She was not surprised. Most of the women in the place had cast looks across at him, whatever their age or marital status.

No wonder he's so full of himself, she thought mordantly. She wondered whether they'd still be lusting after him if they knew he'd threatened her with jail to get her into his bed.

Her face shuttered again. She reached for her water glass.

As she did, she saw that Leo was looking at her. He was frowning slightly, as if he'd been confronted with something unexpected.

Leo went on looking at her. That tiny incident just then, with the child, had taken him aback. Anna had smiled—a warm, kindly smile—clearly charmed by the little girl.

He'd never seen her look like that before. It was—out of character. A side of Anna Delane he hadn't seen—that shouldn't be there. Not in a woman like her.

The waiter arrived with their wine and placed the glasses carefully at their places. Anna, he noticed, took a mouthful immediately.

He took a sip from his and leant back, surveying her.

It was strange to see her away from the villa—with other people. Male eyes were drifting across to her repeatedly, but she wasn't taking any notice. Doubtless for a woman as beautiful as her it was a daily occurrence. Yet, unlike all the other beautiful women he knew, she seemed to radiate absolutely no awareness of male observation. Other women showed they could see it coming their way, and sat there almost preening. Anna simply got on with having lunch.

Was that part of her challenge—that she ignored men who looked at her? Did she do it deliberately? Surely she must. He remembered what had struck him most at the gala launch at the Schloss—that she was completely indifferent to her own beauty.

As he watched her, so extraordinarily beautiful, the object of covert and not so covert male looks, he wondered caustically what they would say if they knew she was a criminal who'd help herself to their belongings without the blink of an eye.

His jaw set. She looked so serenely indifferent, sitting there, ignoring him. As if butter wouldn't melt...

It made him feel like needling her, forgetting his deal to have a civil day together.

'So, not tempted by the coral bracelet, then? Tell me, would you steal from a child if it had something you wanted?'

Anna looked at him. 'That's a stupid and offensive question,' she replied coldly.

'Why? I want to know if there are limits to your venality, that is all. You stole from me, why not from a child?' Leo jibed.

She eyed him stonily.

'A crime is not a crime, *per se*,' she said. 'A crime depends upon motive, and on effect on the victim. Is a starving man entitled to steal food from one who has ten times more than he needs? Supposing he stole it for his starving child, to save its life?'

'You're quite a moralist,' Leo observed, eyes narrowing slightly as he lifted his wine glass to his mouth. 'For a thief.' He took a mouthful of wine. 'I asked you once before why you stole from me, Anna—'

'And I told you it was none of your business. That's still the case.'

Leo started to feel the anger running in him again. But, as their food arrived, his attention was diverted.

'Is that what you ordered?' he asked, eyeing the succulent dish sceptically.

'Yes,' Anna said. 'It's by way of celebration.'

'Celebration?'

She gave her acid-sweet smile. 'My night off,' she told him.

For a second his face darkened, then, with visible effort, he made his expression relax. 'It's good to see you eat sensibly for once.'

Anna glanced up at him, midway into spearing a fat, crispy prawn.

'I've told you—I have no choice. Models all have to be

underweight for their height. It's part of the stupid fake mystique of high fashion.'

Leo began to eat. 'You sound very hostile to your career.'

Anna gave a shrug. 'I just don't have any illusions about it. I never did,' she added reflectively.

'I thought it was a dream come true for most women—to be a model?'

She ate some more, luxuriating in the rich flavours.

'The fashion industry treats models like garbage—remember the charming Signor Embrutti, wanting Jenny to strip off, not giving a toss that she didn't want to? Think that's unusual? Models have to be incredibly tough to survive.'

'That should suit you ideally,' riposted Leo sardonically. 'I also remember you threatening with your contract terms and conditions at Embrutti.'

Her face darkened. 'That slimeball! I've worked with him before, so I insisted that all four models should have a no strip clause as soon as I knew Justin the Obsequious had hired him for the shoot—'

'*What* did you call him?' Leo set down his knife and fork.

'Should I have called him Justin the Toad?' returned Anna limpidly. 'Oh, for heaven's sake, surely you know the man is a total toerag?'

'He is keen to do his job well,' Leo replied quellingly.

'Keen to lick your boots, more like. *Yes, Mr Makarios. Of course, Mr Makarios. Anything you say with spots on, Mr Makarios.*' She looked at him. 'You don't genuinely want to surround yourself with toadies, do you?'

There was a puzzled, incredulous expression on her face.

Leo's mouth tightened and he started to eat again.

'My staff know that I expect—and get—the highest-calibre performances from them. In exchange they are very well paid indeed. As,' he pointed out acidly, 'you and the other models were for the work you did.'

'And we worked our backsides off, believe me! Do you have any complaints about the quality of our work? You saw us in action, after all.'

'No, you were all perfectly professional,' he allowed. 'Even with you threatening contracts at the photographer. You do that often, do you?'

'When I have to. I learnt the hard way. When I was starting out some ad agency creep insisted on bare boob shots. My agency told me to do it. I walked out. It cost me that job, and a lot of work afterwards. From then on I ensured a no strip clause was in every contract I signed.'

Leo was frowning at her.

'Why is it such a big deal? Nudity is nothing these days.'

Anna put down her fork and stared at him.

'OK, so strip off. Go on. Flash yourself around at these good folk here. Put some flesh shots of yourself in a glossy mag. Make sure your friends and relatives see it. Make sure total strangers on the London Underground see it.'

'Do not be absurd!' Leo retorted stiffly. 'You are a fashion model. You—'

Her eyes flashed green fire.

'Yes—I am a *fashion model*,' she spelt out. 'I model clothes. I do not model *not wearing any clothes*. Can you *possibly* understand the subtle difference?'

Leo glared at her. Her aggression was ludicrous—it was absurd—it was insolent—it was—

It was justified.

He took a sharp, deep breath. He flung his hands up as if in surrender.

'I take your point. But,' he went on, genuine puzzlement showing in his eyes, 'if you dislike modelling so much, why did you become one?'

Leo leant back again, lifting his wine glass to his mouth. Anna's eyes followed the movement, watching the way his long, strong fingers curved around the bowl of the wine glass, the way his sensual, mobile mouth indented as he drank. How the strong column of his throat worked as he swallowed.

Weakness ebbed through her, dissolving and debilitating. Dear God, but he was just so beautiful to look at...

She came back with a start.

'Well, however much I moan about it, it still beats packing biscuits all day long in the local factory,' she returned, taking a mouthful of wine herself, to restore her composure. 'I never did well at school, so higher education was out.'

'You don't strike me as unintelligent,' observed Leo. 'Why did you not do well at school?'

She looked at him, surprised. Leo Makarios didn't look like the kind of man to assess any woman for her intelligence. Let alone *her*. Perhaps, she thought acidly, he assumed that a thief had to have a basic degree of intelligence.

'I'll answer that for you,' he said dryly. 'I can't see you taking kindly to a teacher's authority.'

Anna's face was expressive. 'Some were OK,' she allowed. 'But most of them…' She didn't finish the sentence. Then she shrugged. 'But I was the one who was the fool—I should have been smart enough to make school work for me. Instead…' She shrugged again. 'Anyway, when I was eighteen I got spotted by a talent scout for an agency, trawling the shopping malls of north London. That got me started.' She took another mouthful of wine to wash down the spicy prawns. 'My gran—she'd brought me up—hated it. She thought I'd be dragged into a den of iniquity. She was right, of course. But luckily I wised up pretty fast. And toughened up. I don't put up with garbage any more.'

The wine was coiling slowly through her veins in the warmth of the day and the rare pleasure of eating filling food. The combination made her feel strangely relaxed. Maybe that was why she was able to talk like this to Leo Makarios. She took another forkful of food, her eyes flickering to his face. It was odd, definitely, to be talking to him.

Leo contemplated her.

'Are you as aggressive with your lovers?' he enquired.

Anna's fork stopped halfway to her mouth, and lowered again.

'I don't have lovers,' she said tightly.

Leo stared at her.

Anna Delane didn't have lovers?

He wanted to laugh out loud. Of course a woman as beautiful as she was had lovers. Men must have been swarming around her since she hit puberty!

Did that mean she'd helped herself, though? She certainly threw you out of her bedroom, right enough!

He jabbed angrily at the piece of lamb fillet he'd just cut. It always came back to that, didn't it? Anna Delane throwing him out of her bedroom. Spitting with outraged virtue even while her breasts were still taut and aroused from his caressing...

A hypocrite. That was all she was. Saying one thing with her mouth while her body spoke a quite, quite different language...

'What do you mean, you don't have lovers?'

His own question interrupted his thoughts, which were leading him in a direction he did not want to go on a day he'd told her she could have the night to herself.

Anna resumed eating.

'I mean I don't have lovers,' she repeated. 'What's the big deal?'

'Why not?' There was genuine incomprehension in his voice, as well as underlying disbelief at her extraordinary assertion. 'You are far too beautiful not to take lovers.'

The flash of green fire came again. 'You mean I have some sort of duty to offer myself on a plate to all comers just because they fancy me?' Her voice was shrivelling with contempt.

'Of course not. I merely mean that with your looks you could have the pick of my sex.'

Anna's mouth tightened. 'With you as a prime example? No, thanks.' The green flash came again. 'Look, I thought the deal was we were going to try and be civil to each other. So stop going on at me, all right? Can't you talk about the weather or something?'

He sat back. 'Very well,' he said heavily. There was an expression in his eyes she could not read. 'So, what would you like to do after lunch?'

She shrugged. 'You know the island, not me.'

'Would you like to do more shopping?'

She rolled her eyes. 'Good grief, what is it with you? I don't need or want to buy anything else, thank you. Actually—' a thought struck her '—what I do want is a swim, to cool off. Is there a beach nearby?' Another thought struck her. 'But maybe with your ankle you can't go in the water?'

'That is not a problem,' replied Leo airily, astonished that she'd actually condescended to voice a preference to him. 'And I know just the beach to take you to.' His eyes gleamed. 'Tell me, can you surf?'

Anna stared. 'Surf? In the Caribbean? It's flat as a millpond!'

Leo laughed. 'Not on the Atlantic coast, it isn't.'

Nor was it. To Anna's astonishment the wide, sandy beach that Leo drove to after they'd finished lunch curled with breakers rolling in from the east. He parked the car by a small café-bar just on the sand, and Anna slipped into the restrooms to change into one of the two new swimsuits she'd bought that morning. Leo, it seemed, had his trunks on underneath his trousers anyway. As she emerged, she saw him standing on the sand, stripped to the waist, a pair of colourful boogie boards under his arm, newly purchased from a beach vendor.

'Surf's up!' he told Anna, grinning, and handed her a board. Then, turning on his heel, he ran with a limping gait into the water and plunged over a breaking wave. With a sudden, inexplicable burst of exuberance, Anna ran after him and did likewise.

Foaming water burst over her head—cold for a second, and then warm. She gave a shout, and found herself grinning back at Leo, hair slicked back, torso glittering with diamonds.

'Watch out!' he called, as another wave curled towards them. 'Turn around, board to your midriff—wait, wait… Now!' Leo launched forward, catching the wave and creaming in towards the shore, weaving his route between the other surfers and swimmers.

Anna was less lucky, and missed the wave. But she caught the next one, and the exhilaration of being powered effortlessly into shore was intoxicating. The moment she grounded she was up on her feet, ploughing back out to sea to repeat the process, over and over again. Beside her, Leo set the pace relentlessly, exchanging grins with her as the water's power swept them inshore time after time.

Finally, after what seemed like a million waves, Anna beached herself in the shallows, lying on her board, dragging in the ebbing surf. Leo came and flopped beside her.

'I'm done in!' she gasped.

Leo jack-knifed to his feet lithely and held a hand down to her.

'Time for a cool drink,' he said.

Anna took his hand without thinking, letting his strong fingers curl around hers, and got to her feet. He went on holding her hand as they waded ashore, boogie boards under their arms. The sun was hot on their wet skin, the sea dazzling. Gaining the shade of the wooden café-bar was blissful, and Anna flopped down at a table.

'Enjoy it?' asked Leo, flopping likewise.

Anna grinned. 'It was fantastic!'

For a moment their eyes held, with nothing in them except mutual good humour. Then one of the waiting staff undulated over to them, with the characteristically graceful islander gait, and asked what they would like.

'Long, cool, and a lot of fruit juice, please.' Anna smiled at her.

'Twice.' Leo nodded. The woman smiled, and undulated back to the bar, sandals flapping lazily on the ground.

Anna's eyes went after her.

'They walk so gracefully, the islanders. Even when they are no longer young or slim. It's very striking. I can't work out how they do it.'

Leo leant back.

'It's because they never hurry,' he answered. 'It's too hot to hurry. So everyone relaxes.'

Anna gave a crooked smile. 'Wise people,' she commented. 'They know what's important in life.'

'"Getting and spending, we lay waste our powers",' Leo

heard himself murmur, repeating the line of poetry that had come to him when he had been out on the villa's terrace that first night.

Anna's quizzical glance rested on him.

'Somehow that sentiment doesn't go with the hotshot business tycoon,' she said dryly.

Leo's eyelashes swept down. 'Is that how you see me? A hotshot business tycoon?'

'It's how you see yourself,' she riposted.

She expected to see his expression bristle, but instead there was a strange look in his eye.

'It's what was expected of me,' he said slowly. His dark eyes rested on her. 'You escaped your background, Anna. I didn't.'

She frowned, confused. 'Why would you want to—given your background?'

'I grew up with a lot of physical riches—but not much else.'

A snort escaped her. 'Poor little rich boy?'

'How close were you to your grandmother?' he asked, ignoring her sceptical comment.

She looked away a moment. 'Very. She was all I had. My mother died when I was five, and as for my father—well, even the child maintenance people couldn't find him. So it was just Gran and me. Which is a lot more than some kids get in life, so I'm not ungrateful, believe me. But sometimes it was…' She paused.

Something looked different in Leo's face.

'Lonely?' he supplied.

Her expression changed.

'Yes,' she admitted.

'So was I,' he said. He saw her disbelief and went on. 'Oh, there was a houseful of servants—several housefuls!—but my parents didn't bother with me. My father was a workaholic and my mother a society queen. I only became interesting to them when I was old enough to be put to work in an office or tout around socially to catch the interest of young women with commercially and politically influential fathers.'

There was a cynical note in his voice that Anna would have had to be deaf not to hear. But her ear heard something else as well. Something she would never in a million years have associated with someone as sublimely pleased with themselves as Leo Makarios.

It was sadness.

Something moved in her. She did not know what, but it disturbed her.

Made her want to reach across the table.

Take his hand.

Almost, almost, she felt her hand move. Then, with an effort of will, she halted it. Leo Makarios was nothing to her. Nothing except a man tormenting her, night after night, with the hopeless, helpless, shameful desires of her own body.

And yet—

The waitress reappeared, with graceful motion, carrying two tall glasses full of crushed ice and a blend of orange and scarlet juice. Anna was grateful for the diversion—and the quenching drink after so much salty water.

She sipped thirstily through the straw as Leo did likewise.

Then she sat back, lifting her damp, drying hair from her neck.

'It's still so hot!' she exclaimed, arching her throat.

Leo's eyes were riveted to her. He could not help it. The gesture she was making was so unconsciously sensual—her slender arms lifted, her swelling breasts thrust upwards by the movement, her long, loose tousled hair, the languorous tilt of her throat—that his breath caught in his body.

Thee mou, but she is beauty incarnate...

A wave of emotion went through him. It was desire. He knew it must be.

But it was more—what he could not say, could not name. But it was strong, and powerful.

And very, very disturbing.

Abruptly, he pushed his empty glass away from him and got to his feet.

'Time to go,' he said.

*   *   *

'Damn, I've caught the sun!'

Anna examined the skin on her forearm.

Leo glanced away from the road for a moment as they drove away from the beach.

'You haven't burnt, don't worry. A light tan will only flatter you.'

She made a face.

'One of my selling points is my pale skin. I try never to tan—even on a tropical shoot. Oh, well.' She shrugged. 'Too late now.'

It was, too, but somehow she couldn't bring herself to care much about losing her ivory skin tones. After everything else that was happening to her, it seemed very trivial. She brushed off the sheen of salt crystallising on her skin. 'I need a shower,' she said.

Leo kept his eye on the pitted road. Nobly, he forbore to suggest that she take one with him. He even tried extremely hard—and failed—to stop his imagination supplying the details. Imagination, he found, was quite enough to make his body react in hopeful anticipation. Uncomfortably, he shifted in the driving seat. He kept his gaze doggedly ahead. Hell, he must have been insane to make the deal he had at lunchtime—letting Anna have a night on her own.

His eyes narrowed.

And yet—and yet it was extraordinarily pleasant to have their armistice. Have Anna lose her dogged, resentful hostility towards him even for this short interlude.

But why should it just be for an interlude? Why not for as long as we are here?

The thought came unbidden, and took hold.

The afternoon had been good. They had passed it in inconsequential conversation, with him talking about the island, her asking the kind of questions any visitor would ask. And as for that spontaneous surfing session, it had been—

Fun, that was what it had been. The word was the only one that fitted.

A sense of astonishment filled him. Of all the experiences

he might have imagined with Anna Delane, having fun—bois-
terous, seaside fun—was the very last he would ever have
thought of.

But fun it had been. Simple, uncomplicated, almost childlike
fun…

He eased back in his driving seat. Well-being suffused
through him. At his side, Anna's silence no longer seemed
aggressive and adversarial—just…peaceful.

He went on driving, heading west into the lowering sun.

Anna was drying her freshly washed hair when Leo knocked
on her bedroom door and walked in. For a brief moment his
eyes flickered over her in a way she was hotly familiar with.
She felt a flush of heat go through her body but crushed it
back. This was her night off. She'd earned it. Earned it being
'civil' to Leo Makarios all afternoon. Doing that definitely deserved a reward!

Except—her memory skidded back along the previous
hours—it had not exactly proved an ordeal. The afternoon, she
could not help but admit with her habitual honesty, had been—
OK.

More than OK. In fact, it had been—

She bit her lip, unwilling to let her mind supply the word it
wanted to.

Good. It had been good.

Enjoyable. Relaxing. Fun. Nice. Easy.

The words ran on, disturbing her even more than the way
Leo's eyes were flickering over her towel-wrapped body.

'Yes?' she prompted.

'We've been invited out to dinner tonight,' Leo said. 'By
one of the government ministers responsible for inward investment. Wear something relaxed, but chic. Do you have anything suitable?'

'I dare say I can manage,' said Anna dryly.

That she had succeeded was evident from the expression in
Leo's eyes when she went downstairs an hour or so later. The
red silk skirt and top were vivid, yet the loose cut on her tall,

slender body gave her a languorous elegance that matched the semi-pinned knot of her long, tendrilled hair. Her matching sandals were low-heeled, and her jewellery was a gold torque and matching bracelets. Her make up was subtle.

'You look fantastic,' breathed Leo.

She gave him a polite, social smile, but it flickered uncertainly on her face.

Although she had been apprehensive about the evening, it proved easy enough. While the minister talked tax and finance to Leo, his wife engaged Anna in conversation. With the poise she had acquired in her years since leaving home, Anna chatted pleasantly to her hostess.

By the time his chauffeur-driven car was whisking them homeward, Leo was in a very good mood. The minister had been encouraging about his property development plans, and as for Anna, she had clearly charmed her hosts with her natural, unaffected manner. A memory came back to him, of Anna conversing with Hans Federman at Schloss Edelstein—obviously not in the least bothered that he was dull and middle-aged. His house staff liked her too, he could tell—but then she had an easy air with everyone, he realised.

Even, tonight, with him.

She was asking him now about his villa development in the south.

'It's a complex of villas and low-rise condominiums on one of the undeveloped promontories,' he answered. 'The government are concerned that the site will not be over-exploited. Water, too, is an issue on the island, which has no large rivers, so the villas have to be designed with water conservation in mind.'

Anna let him run on. He was clearly enthusiastic about the project, and knowledgeable too. Every now and then she asked prompting questions.

'I'll take you down tomorrow and show you,' he finished, as the car finally wheeled through the gates of his villa.

'OK,' she answered easily.

She went back into the cool of the villa. Memory slipped

back to her—the first night she'd got here, tired and jet-lagged, with a hard, tight knot inside her stomach at the reason she was there.

It seemed, she realised as she walked indoors, a long time ago.

Much longer than the number of days she'd been here.

At her side, Leo caught up, even with his limping gait.

'How's the ankle?' she heard herself ask.

Leo grimaced. 'A damn nuisance—but it has its compensations.' He glanced down at her. 'Like you asking about it,' he murmured.

She gave a half-dismissive, half-embarrassed shrug at having been caught out expressing solicitude.

'Coffee?' he asked.

Anna nodded. 'Thank you, that would be nice.'

They walked out onto the terrace and Anna took her place on the lounger beside the coffee table, looking out over the softly lit pool. In her veins she felt the wine of the evening making her feel relaxed and sleepy. On the other lounger, Leo was resting his bad ankle.

'How did you do it?' Anna heard herself asking as she helped herself to coffee. Without thinking, she poured out a cup for Leo as well, and handed it to him.

'I fell off my windsurf board, like a complete novice,' he answered in self-disgust, taking the cup from her.

She gave a wry smile. 'I don't know how anyone stays on those things anyway,' she commented.

Leo took a mouthful of hot coffee and twisted his head towards her.

'If you can ride a bike you can windsurf. It's not that hard. I'll teach you.'

Anna felt her fingers clench around the cup handle.

'I think I'll pass. My insurance policy doesn't allow me to do dangerous sports.' She kept her voice deliberately light, as though the prospect of being taught windsurfing by the man keeping her in his bed by blackmail was nothing much.

'You are insured?' Leo's voice sounded surprised.

'Against loss of earnings from injury. It seemed a prudent thing to do.'

'Prudent?' echoed Leo. *Prudent?* A woman who thought nothing of stealing a ruby bracelet wasn't someone he'd call prudent. A frown creased his brow. Today had shown him a new side to Anna Delane—as if she were just a normal person, instead of a criminal.

His eyes went to her as she looked out over the beach. The evening had been so good, the day so good, and he knew exactly how he wanted it to end. Anna looked so fantastic, long-limbed, beautiful, with the grace that took his breath away every time.

Emotion rose in him. It was desire, he knew it was—intense and piercing, making him want to get to his feet, sweep her up into his arms and find the nearest bedroom. It was a familiar feeling, one that came over him every night.

But there was something unfamiliar mingled in with desire. He searched for a moment, then gave up. It wasn't anger, that was for sure, or exasperation, or annoyance, or any of the other frustrations that Anna Delane's cussedness towards him always aroused. But what it was he had no idea. And because he couldn't identify it, he put it aside. Right now he wasn't interested. Right now there was only one thing he was interested in.

He took another mouthful of coffee, then put the cup down.

'Have you finished your coffee?' he asked. His voice had a husk in it.

Anna's head swivelled round to him. Leo reached out his hand and smoothed it along her bare arm. Her skin was warm to the touch, as soft as the silk of her dress. His blood quickened at the touch; his eyelashes swept down over his darkening eyes. In his veins desire creamed, rich with anticipation.

She was just so beautiful, so desirable…

But even as his eyes rested on her, appreciating her delectable body, Anna's expression was changing. Freezing.

He could feel her—see her—pulling away mentally and physically.

'You said,' she enunciated, 'I could have the night off.'

It was like a slap with a wet towel. His hand drew back instantly.

And in the same instant the old, familiar flare of sheer exasperated anger shot through him.

He gave a short, heavy sigh.

'Don't tell me—it's in your contract,' he said grimly.

'It was a verbal contract,' she answered.

Leo's eyes flashed. 'You missed your vocation—you should have been a lawyer. Instead of a thief,' he reminded her nastily.

Her face tightened. 'You said I could have the night off,' she repeated doggedly.

Angrily, Leo reached for his coffee again.

'Do what you want,' he said moodily, and took another mouthful. He wished it were brandy, so he could drink himself into oblivion. His body didn't seem to want to be accepting of Anna's rejection of him. He shifted restlessly.

'Try a cold shower,' he heard her say coolly.

He flashed a killing look at her.

Then went back to staring moodily into the night.

Damn Anna Delane. And damn himself for wanting her so much.

He thrust his cup aside again, and got to his feet. This was hopeless—he couldn't sit there with her beside him, rejecting him.

'I'll see you at breakfast,' he announced bleakly, and limped inside.

Out on the terrace, Anna sat still. It was her turn to stare moodily into the sub-tropical darkness.

Her turn to damn both herself and him. And, worst of all, to damn the desire he had quickened in her, which she was forcing down now with every ounce of her will-power lest it overpower her and send her running hungrily, desperately, after him.

CHAPTER NINE

THE project manager at Leo Makarios's development complex was telling her about the different kinds of hardwood used in construction of the villas, but Anna was hardly paying attention. She was far too conscious of Leo's presence beside her—much too aware of his edgy mood—and of her own.

Instead of luxuriating in an undisturbed night in her own bed she had slept badly, restless and interrupted. Now she felt heavy-eyed and bleary, but running with a tense energy.

Her mood was bleak. A truth was pressing at her that she didn't want to accept—mustn't accept. Her eyes slid past the half-constructed villas out over the endless seas beyond, and a hollow misery filled her. Oh, God, how had it come to this? Tossing and turning all night, staring blindly up at the ceiling, unable to find any peace, any repose—all for the sake of Leo Makarios?

Her eyes hardened beneath the concealing veil of her dark glasses. She had to fight this—she had to. It was nothing but a sick weakness—a stupid, unforgivable, temporary insanity. Nothing else. And she would overcome it! She had to—she just had to...

At her side the project manager had turned his attention to his employer, drawing his notice to something on the sheaf of architectural drawings in his hand. With half an ear Anna heard Leo's deep voice answering brusquely, his voice edged like a serrated knife.

When they left the site she was relieved, and yet it was even worse being incarcerated in the car alone with Leo. He did not speak to her, nor she to him, yet the silent tension between them pulled at her, making her muscles tense in mental resistance. Her hands pressed into each other in her lap. Her throat felt constricted.

He drove for a good half an hour, over twisting coastal roads, until he turned into a private drive that led down to the sea—a low-rise beach hotel his destination.

'Lunch,' he announced tersely, and got out of the car. Silently Anna followed suit, and went into the hotel with him.

She disliked it immediately. It was clearly a boutique hotel, aimed at a clientele bored with mundane tourism and demanding a novelty of design that Anna castigated as pretentious. So was the menu.

'A vegetarian salad, please,' she ordered. 'No dressing.'

'I thought you were starting to eat normally?' said Leo edgily.

Anna shrugged. 'The prices are ludicrous and the menu idiotic.'

Leo's eyes narrowed. 'This is rated as one of the best hotels in the Caribbean.'

Anna stared at him. 'The décor is pretentious, the staff snooty, and the guests are all posers. That place yesterday was a million times better.'

'Well, we're here now,' Leo returned, and moodily studied the wine list.

'Just mineral water for me—sparkling,' said Anna.

'I'm glad something is,' he retorted.

They ate in virtual silence, Leo grim-faced and Anna tense. Had they really been having an almost normal conversation just twenty-four hours ago? she wondered disbelievingly. Now she could hardly say two words to him. Not that he seemed in the mood for conversation. She was grateful. All she wanted now was to get out of here, back to the villa, and lock herself in her bedroom. Or anywhere. She felt jittery, restless. Looking anywhere but at Leo.

And yet somewhere deep inside her it was as if an electric charge were building, dangerously overloading her nerves. Her muscles were tense, her skin prickling. Her body seemed alive, but in an alien, uncontrolled way, as if it wanted something—

something that she must not, would not think about. Her fingers tightened around her fork, she held her neck rigid, so she could not let herself look across at the man sitting opposite her. A man who seemed as restless, as on edge, as she was.

Her teeth clenched. She would not look across at him. She *would* not.

Doggedly she went on eating, though the food tasted like sawdust for all its exorbitant price.

Inside her, coiling tighter and tighter, the electric charge went on building. Silently.

Dangerously.

The meal crawled to its interminable end. Leo seemed determined to drag it out, ordering a dessert and then coffee, when all she wanted to do was jerk to her feet and get out—out of here, away from him.

The tension radiating from him was palpable.

Finally, when she thought she must just scrape her chair back and rush off, he pushed aside his empty coffee cup.

'Anna—'

His voice was edged, serrated. It had been like that all morning. But now it was worse.

Her jaw tightened. She said nothing.

'Look at me.'

What was it in his voice that made her do it? Let her eyes off the leash she had been pinning them down with. Let them lift and meet the dark, heavy-lidded eyes fastening on her.

Electricity cracked through her, the charge arcing across to his eyes.

Telling him exactly, *exactly*, what he wanted to know…

'No.' Her voice was low. *'No!'*

She jerked to her feet—the way every tense, coiled muscle was impelling her to.

Leo followed suit, his hand impatiently, imperiously beckoning for the bill. When the waiter glided over, Leo had his card at the ready. As he handed it over, scrawling his name on the chit, he said something in a low voice to the man, who nodded without a flicker of his eyes. He glided away with the credit card while Anna stood, tension racking through every limb, then returned, handing back the card to Leo—and something else besides. She did not see what it was and did not care. She knew only that she must, *must* get out of here. It was imperative. Essential.

'Let's go,' said Leo, and headed off. His voice sounded harsh, but Anna ignored it. She just wanted to get out of there, the quickest way, and she followed his rapid stride from the dining room without complaint.

But he didn't lead the way back out to the front of the hotel. Instead he went down into the gardens. Shrugging mentally, Anna followed him. She could see palm-fronded beach cottages artfully sited amongst the banana trees and cultivated vegetation, and beyond them the white of the beach backed by the azure of the sea… Without realising it, she saw that she had followed Leo along a paved path and up to the door of one of the cottages. He held the door open for her.

Did he want to change for a swim? she wondered, stepping inside. She could do with one—maybe it would help to drain off this relentless feeling of edgy, restless tension netting her body. She turned to tell him that her swimsuit was in the car.

And froze.

Leo was looking at her.

Looking at her through heavy-lidded eyes focused totally and absolutely upon her. With an expression in them that told her that swimming was the very last thing on his mind.

And instantly, like an electric arc between them, she felt her body flaring. Her heart-rate surged and her breath came raggedly as the hunger she had been fighting all morning suddenly, urgently, took her over. Completely, absolutely.

She couldn't move. Could only stand there, frozen, as he pressed the door shut with the palm of his hand and moved slowly, purposefully, towards her.

He didn't speak, nor she. He only stood for a timeless moment in front of her, and then his hands were spearing into her hair, either side of her head, and his mouth was slanting down over hers.

She opened to him, blood igniting, hunger and desire leaping in her as she twined her mouth with his.

Oh, God, it was bliss! She wanted more, more of him. Now—right now. Her body pressed against his, her breasts swelling and tautening, and she could feel his body respond. The excitement of it ripped through her.

'*Christos*—Anna—'

Leo's voice was harsh, jagged, and then it was cut off as his mouth returned to devour hers. She gave a low moan, wrapping her arms around him, feeling the glory of his hard muscled back beneath her cleaving fingers. She wanted him. Wanted him so much, so intensely, that she felt faint with it. Her body was starving, ravenous for him—deprived of him, of what he could do to her, for a whole agonising long day and night.

Her nipples were hard against his torso, and the sensation aroused yet more and more wanting in her. She pressed her hips against him, feeling his surging masculine response, and she moaned again low in her throat as her mouth mated with his in avid, ravening hunger. Desire and excitement were ripping through her, tearing like a knife, demanding to be sated and slaked on him—*him*—Leo Makarios, whose body she craved, *needed*, now…right now…

Leo's hands had left her hair, had slid down her flanks, curving around the soft mounds of her bottom, lifting her into him so that he could intensify the sensation at the vee of her legs, pressed against his strong, erect manhood. Instinctively she lifted her knee, using her thigh to caress his, winding her foot around his calf, rubbing his leg with hers, her skirts hoisting high.

He was moving her, twisting her around, backing her towards the wide, inviting expanse of the bed, where he could take her, free their bodies of their useless restricting clothes and slake their devouring need for physical satiation.

For a few blinded seconds she surfaced for air, taking a deep, gulping breath to fill her ragged lungs, blood coursing hotly through her veins, her body on fire with desire for him, desperate for him, starving for him...

A shadow of movement stilled her. In the dim light of the shaded interior she suddenly saw a pair of figures outlined in the silvered mirror on the wall.

Writhing, abandoned...out of all control except for the urges of their raw sexuality.

It was like a douche of cold water over her heated body.

She wrenched away, staring, appalled, at the reflection.

Cold, sick horror drenched through her.

What am I doing?

The words seared in her head, and she did not need a translation.

She took a stumbling step backwards.

'Anna—' Leo was reaching for her again, his voice hoarse.

Her eyes flared.

'Don't touch me!'

His expression darkened. 'What the hell—?'

She took another step back.

'I said, don't touch me.'

Mortification was flooding through her, and hot, humid shame. Oh, God, had it come to this? Being bundled into a hotel room for a quick, urgent session of sexual satiation? A room hired by the hour. And afterwards, when he'd slaked himself on her, he'd tell her to get dressed again, and he would do likewise, body sated, and then he'd walk out beside her, his hand under her elbow—the woman he'd just had sex with in a hotel room after lunch—and put down his credit card at the desk to pay for his pleasure, rented by the hour...

She couldn't bear it.

Anguish sheared through her. And shame and anger.

He stepped towards her, his hands reaching out for her.

She stepped further away.

'I don't want this.'

Her voice was high, staccato. Strung on a wire, pulled taut. Unbearably taut.

Something moved in his face.

'Liar—'

His voice was low, eyes intent. Slowly, deliberately, he reached for her.

'Anna Delane—you are a liar to tell me you don't want this. Don't want *me*.'

Leo's hand closed around her wrist, drawing her to him.

She could not resist him. Her breathing quickened again, eyes dilating, heat flushing through her. Oh, God, she wanted this all right! Wanted him...

Leo felt her relax, felt the resistance ebb from her. Felt her go weak, the way he wanted her to be—weak with desire for him. Only for him. Now. Right now.

He started to slide his hands around her waist, to take her back in his arms, feel her soft, slim body pliant against his.

The blow took him entirely by surprise. And in that moment, as Anna drew her arm back with whip-like reaction from where the side of her hand had impacted on his upper arm, she pulled away from him.

Leo stared, disbelieving. She was standing there, in a martial arts fighting pose, balanced on the balls of her feet, one arm drawn back, elbow crooked and her hand fisted loosely at her hip, the other arm extended, warding him off, palm facing him.

'I said no,' she told him.

Her face was set. Only her eyes flared. Showing something in them he would not recognise. Refused to recognise.

'What the hell,' Leo said slowly, 'are you doing?'

She drew her breath in sharply.

'I don't want this. I don't want sex with you now. I don't want sex with you now, here, in a hotel room that you've just tipped a waiter to open up for you. Just because you're in the mood—'

His mouth twisted. 'Anna. Do you think you faked your reaction just now? Like hell you did. You want it, and you've wanted it since last night, when you said no to me and then regretted it and were too damn stubborn to admit it. You've been wanting it all day—that's why you lit up like a volcano just now. The way you always do—always have done with me—every, every time. So don't come the hypocrite with me, Anna Delane, because we both know you want me—you want everything I give you! Everything you give me!'

Leo took a step towards her. Deliberately. Clear intent in his face.

Anger stabbed through her, like a knife slicing through a curtain. Vicious and violent. It had come out of nowhere, like a summer storm boiling out of the sky.

Taking her over.

Taking her over completely.

She felt its power surge through her, coruscating, burning. Released like a tiger, pouring through her.

'I don't *give* you sex at all!' she hissed back at him. 'You *take* it! You take it! And I won't. I *won't* be reduced to having quick, sordid sex like you want now!'

Dark eyes flashed in unleashed fury.

'Sordid?' Leo snarled. His face blackened. 'Do I have to remind you,' he bit out—and there was something in his voice that suddenly made Anna feel sick— 'why you are here at all on this island, with me? You're a thief—a criminal!'

'And so are you.'

'Are you insane?' he demanded.

It was his incredulity that did it for her. Sent the anger searing through her again. She knew she should not let it take over. Knew that, poised like this, her body both her weapon and her defence, she should hold the calm, the dispassion, the control that her sensei would insist on.

But she couldn't. She couldn't control anything.

Let alone her anger. It was coursing through her—destructive, burning.

'You're blackmailing me into sex with you, threatening me with jail, and that makes you a criminal.'

His hand slashed through the air.

'*Thee mou*—I keep you out of jail and you call that *threatening* you?' There were white lines incised around his mouth. His eyes were hard, hard as iron. Black iron. 'I will not have you twist the truth into your own fantasy!' Greek burst from him, staccato and rabid. 'I have taken all I am prepared to take from you. Your stubborn, shameless refusal to show the slightest sign of guilt, or remorse, or contrition for what you did. You spit and snarl at me, *refusing* to acknowledge your crime. And now, *now* you dare to try and accuse me of criminal behaviour?' More Greek broke from him. And a mask came down over his face. She could see it happening. Control. Total self-control of his emotions.

'Put your shoes on. Pick up your bag. We're going.'

He strode to the door, yanking it open. Anna could hear him striding down the path with heavy tread.

Slowly, very slowly, she came out of her blocking stance. Her body was starting to tremble. She felt cold and shaky.

Her breathing shallow, she stooped to gather her bag, her sandals, and then, with a strange, eerie sense of complete emotional dissociation, she left the cottage.

They drove back to the villa in silence. A silence so tangible it could have been cut from a knife.

At the villa, he pulled up at the front entrance.

'Go in,' he instructed.

She got down from the car, but had hardly closed the door when it took off again, pounding back down the drive towards the gate in a swirl of gravel. Slowly she started to move towards the front door.

'Miss Delane?'

The voice that spoke came from one side, and she turned. A man was walking up to her. He had a steady gait that was somehow menacing. A stab of unease went through Anna in her heightened state of excess emotion.

'Who wants to know?' she countered. She looked to the villa. There was no one around—not even a gardener in the gardens. The man approaching her was a stranger.

A car started moving from where it had been parked, in shadow, at the place where the drive swept away round to the garages at the side of the villa. It was black, with tinted windows.

'You will come with me,' the man approaching her said.

Anna backed away. Fear was running in her. What the hell was going on? Why were there no house staff around? She made to turn and run inside, to find someone—anyone.

Her arm was seized. A vice lock.

Automatically she lashed out, striking down at the man's open side. But even as the side of her hand impacted he moved, coming round the back of her and striking her with a blow that all but knocked her out. Before she could recover she was being pushed, head-first, inside the car, thrust face down on the floor, so she could scarcely breathe, hardly think, hardly believe what was happening to her. There were voices—harsh, urgent—the car jerked forward, its engine revving. She tried to surface, fight through the terror buckling through her, but she was thrust back down again, a foot painful on her neck. Darkness rolled over her.

Leo stood, staring out to sea. He was on a rocky headland, where a rough track led to the ruins of an eighteenth-century British fort.

He could still feel anger coursing through him.

Of course it was anger. What else could it be? It was the only thing he was feeling. Burning, biting anger.

Anger at Anna Delane.

Criminal. Thief. Hypocrite.

Who had dared, *dared* to smear her crime on him. Dared to accuse him—*him*—of being a criminal—a blackmailer. Dared to look down her hypocritical nose and accuse him of being sordid.

Just because he'd wanted her so much, needed her right away—

She wanted it as much as I did. Thee mou, *can I not tell exactly when she is aroused, and how much, and—?*

His mobile phone went off. Impatiently he yanked it from his hip pocket and answered it.

'Yes?' he bit out.

He stilled totally as the caller started speaking.

*   *   *

The knife-blade glinted in the light. The man holding it looked at it, and then at Anna.

'You know, Miss Delane, you would be well advised not to withhold the information I wish to have.'

He rotated the blade, so again it caught the light streaming through the windows.

'You are very beautiful,' he said in his accented English. 'It would be a great pity to ruin that beauty. Now, consider your answer carefully. I ask you once again—where is your friend, Jennifer Carson?'

'I don't know.'

Anna's voice was a thread. She had read in a thriller one time that fear was something you had to experience to believe. And now she believed.

The boat she was on rocked slightly over a wave as it continued to head out to sea, and the man holding her arms behind her back shifted his weight to rebalance. The movement caused renewed pressure on her joints, her shoulders. She felt faint again with the pain, her head muzzy, her brain fogged.

And the fear.

It was in every cell of her body. Like a cancer. In every cell.

The man interrogating her had eyes without expression in them.

'I—I told you,' she said again, her voice almost inaudible. 'She went back to London when I left Austria with Leo Makarios. I don't know where she is now. I don't know anything.'

The man twisted the knife in the sunlight again and it flashed. Anna stared at it with a sick terror.

'I am sure, Miss Delane,' said the man with no expression in his eyes, 'that that is an answer you should reconsider.'

He walked up to her, lifting the knife to her cheek and laying the blade flat. She could feel it pressing against her skin.

'All I have to do,' he told her, 'is twist the blade inwards.'

The sickness churned in her stomach. Her eyes were distended, incapable of focus. Her brain was incapable of thought.

Only of terror.

The man holding her said something to the man with the knife. The latter gave a coarse laugh and pulled the blade from her face. He said something to the first man, and they both laughed. Then the first man looked at Anna again.

'Marking you would lower the price we'd get for you—but there are other ways to make you tell us what we want to know. Pain that will not scar...'

The pit of Anna's stomach dissolved.

'I don't know any more than I've told you,' she whispered. Her eyes were blind with fear.

Then, in the mindless terror that possessed her, she heard something. A faint roaring sound in the distance, over and above the noise of the engine of the boat she was on.

Coming closer.

The man with the knife swore, throwing more words at the man holding Anna, and then strode out onto the open rear deck of the motor yacht she'd been taken aboard by her captors.

Then another sound penetrated her stricken brain.

The steady thud-thud-thud of helicopter rotors.

The man on the stern deck jerked his head upwards, staring around to locate the source. Then his eyes went back out to sea.

Anna fought to try and make her eyes focus, but she couldn't make her muscles work. She couldn't make anything work. Terror was eating at her, taking over her body, shutting out everything else.

The man on the stern deck turned and shouted something to the man holding Anna. The noise of a powerboat engine came closer, and so did the thudding of the helicopter rotors. Anna felt the cruiser they were on start to rock more as the approaching helicopter started its descent, whipping up the waves.

The man with the knife spoke to Anna sneeringly.

'Don't get your hopes up, whore. No one can touch us. Not if they want you alive, that is.' His face changed, become a mask of hatred. 'We'll put you to work in a brothel, where you belong!' He strode up to her, and with a sudden violent move-ment his hand closed over the material of her dress at the bodice and tore it down, exposing her completely. He gave an ugly laugh.

Then suddenly an amplified voice was booming down over the yacht. Anna could not hear the words. Even if she had not been half-dead from fear and pain, she could not have made them out.

The man with the knife strode back to the stern deck and threw his head up, yelled something up at the hovering helicopter.

Out beyond the cruiser's wake, Anna could see another boat approaching. Was that the power boat she had heard? It was closing fast, curving out and round, on an intercepting course to head off her abductors. It was coming closer now. Her eyes twisted to the wide windows lining the side of the cabin. She could see what could only be uniformed police aboard, and then the boat was forcing the yacht to shift to port. She felt their speed slow, jolting her sideways, and the jerking movement on her pinioned arms sent new waves of black pain through her.

Their boat stopped, its churning wake at the rear subsiding to a mere idling. The noise of the rotors increased proportionately, but not enough to drown the amplified voice directed at them—not from the helicopter now, but from the police craft hovering threateningly across the cruiser's starboard bow.

The man on the stern deck shouted something harshly to the man holding her. Anna was jerked forward, forced to go towards the open stern deck.

As she emerged into the brightness she suddenly felt something hard and cold jammed under her ear.

It was the barrel of a gun.

This far out to sea the water was cold as Leo slipped silently into its depths. He ignored it. Blocked out everything except the icy purpose that filled him. Had filled him ever since his blood had run cold when the villa's security head had told him that three gunmen had been holding the house staff at gunpoint, threatening to kill them, and that Anna had been abducted the moment he'd driven off, leaving her at the villa.

The hour that had passed since then had been a living nightmare. The police had been scrambled, but Leo had refused to stay ashore. He and two of his security people had piled into the fastest motor boat he possessed, and headed off in pursuit. A car had been abandoned at the jetty in the next village along the coast, and the villagers there had reported seeing three men drag a young white woman aboard a gleaming cruiser moored, untypically, at the fishermen's jetty. It had left in a roaring wake, heading south.

Cold had drenched through him. This island was one of the safest in the Caribbean—the government extremely protective of its citizens and tourists—especially their very rich ones. So Leo had allowed his personal security at the villa to be minimal.

Too minimal.

Christos—just who the hell had Anna got herself involved with? Who had taken her? And why? The gunmen had been Middle Eastern. That was all his staff had been able to tell him. They had spoken only English. The boat they were using, however, was registered to a South American country.

Drugs? Was that what Anna was involved with? God, he'd known she was a criminal, but stealing priceless jewellery was a world away from drug-running.

Or was it? The criminal underworld was a sick mirror image of the business world—making money out of anything and everything.

Why had his Anna been taken?

He pushed the question from him. It was irrelevant now. Everything was irrelevant except what he was doing. The helicopter-induced swell was running against him, chopping the water and slowing him down, but at least it meant that for the few moments when he had to surface for air he was hidden. The police boat had stopped the cruiser in its tracks, and that and the hovering helicopter were taking all the gunmen's attention.

Getting aboard amidships, well away from the stern deck and the trimmed but still deadly propeller, took all his strength. For a moment he crouched, breathing heavily, just inside the ship's rail, hidden by the bulk of the upper cabin. Then, slowly, he moved.

The man at the wheel was holding the boat as steady as he could in the buffeting from the helicopter, at which he was gazing upwards balefully, as well as keeping his eyes on the police gunmen trained on him from the boat all but grazing his starboard bow. He never even heard Leo in the din.

Cautiously, Leo started to climb up onto the roof of the cabin, sliding along it on his belly. He twisted his head sideways, shaking it warningly at the police on board the boat. Not by a movement or a gesture did they reveal they had seen him. The booming voice from the megaphone was still ordering the gunmen to hand their prisoner over. Somewhere, dimly, he could hear their leader shouting his sneering defiance, telling the police helicopter that if they fired the girl would be dead first. The backs of all three of them were towards Leo, but he could see, with a sick coldness inside him, the gun jammed under Anna's ear. He also saw, with a rage that seared through him like a white heat, that they'd stripped her to the waist.

Silently, like death, he dropped down onto the rear deck.

In a blur, Anna saw the figure drop. For a second terror screamed in her, and then somewhere, in a synapse deep in her brain, she realised who it was.

It was Leo.

Leo—dropping down, pummelling into the man holding the gun to her throat, knocking him to the deck. Anna screamed. And then, from nowhere, she acted. Every muscle in her body went limp and she sagged forward.

Fire shot through her shoulders as they took the full weight of her body, but she didn't care. The change in weight distribution had unbalanced her captor. She hooked her foot around his ankle and, every muscle tensing again, she jerked. He went flying down, almost taking her with him, but at the last moment he released her to try and stop himself hitting the deck. She was on him in a second. Her arms would not work, but her legs would, and she laid in to him, kicking viciously anywhere and everywhere she could to keep him down.

Then, suddenly, she was swept up. Before she could even struggle again she registered that it was Leo—Leo bundling her over the side guardrail of the deck into the waiting arms of one of his security people in the power boat that had come alongside. She heard Leo yell something, and the boat veered off.

'Leo!' She screamed his name, but it could not be heard above the roaring engine.

The police helicopter had shifted, shadowing over the yacht, and she could see two marksmen taking aim from the interior. The swoop of the rotors was ploughing the sea into a frenzy.

The gunman had staggered to his feet, lifting his gun while backing Leo into the cabin, taking aim from the rocking platform. Even through the deafening noise she heard the crack of gunshots, saw Leo launching himself sideways, downwards. Then there were more shots. The police marksmen had shot the gunman and the man was reeling, falling in hideous slow motion, backwards over the churning propellers.

She twisted her head away, hearing yet more shots.

Then no more.

'Leo,' she moaned, 'Oh, God, Leo…'

He was lying motionless, face down on the rocking, jerking deck, and she could see blood staining his shirt. Horror drenched through her.

Leo was dead. He had died saving her.

Grief tore at her like a ravening wolf. Eating her alive.

Then, into the horror, she heard the voice of Leo's security man.

'I think I just saw his hand move!'

CHAPTER TEN

ANNA sat in the waiting room. It was cool. Overhead, a fan rotated slowly. Even with painkillers her wrenched arms and shoulders ached. She didn't care. She didn't care about anything.

Only one thing occupied her entire being.

Leo.

She stared at the clock. How long had he been in Theatre? She didn't know. Knew only that no one was saying reassuring things to her. No one was telling her it was going to be all right.

No one was telling her he was going to live.

My fault. My fault. My fault.

The words tolled through her.

Over and over again.

As she waited, and prayed.

There had been only one other thing she had done since the doctor had discharged her. She had begged the favour of a call to the UK. Across the ocean she had spoken to Jenny, warning her to lie low, that the man who had got her pregnant was prepared to kill for her.

She went on staring at the clock.

My fault. My fault. My fault.

The doors opened. A doctor came out in Theatre garb. He came up to Anna, loosening his mask. His face was grave.

Her throat had a noose around it.

The surgeon looked at her a moment. Then a tired smile formed on his mouth.

'You've got a very tough man there. I've patched him together again, but he needs a reward for all his heroics. Make sure you're there when he surfaces. He deserves a beautiful woman to wake up to.'

Anna burst into tears.

Leo was so pale.

His face like marble.

He hardly seemed to be breathing, and yet the low rise and fall of his bandaged chest told her that he was alive. Blessedly, blessedly alive.

Gratitude flooded through her.

And more, so much more than gratitude.

Shakily, she sat down on a chair and pulled it closer to him. His hands lay on either side of him, inert, pale.

She slid her fingers around the hand nearest her.

Living flesh.

Slowly she lowered her cheek to his hand.

It was wet with tears.

How long she sat there, she did not know. Nurses looked in every now and then—sometimes at her, sometimes to check Leo. The night wore on, and still she sat there, his hand clasped tight in hers, never letting him go.

The dawn came, fingers of pale light stealing into the room. A nurse came to check him again, bringing coffee and sandwiches for Anna.

'His pulse is stronger,' she told her. 'He'll be back with us very soon.' She glanced down at where Anna was holding his hand. 'Don't you let go, now. He knows, you know. You hang on in there.' She gave a last smile. 'Now, drink this coffee while it's hot. And eat.'

She glided out.

Anna went on holding on.

Does he know? Does he know I'm here?

And, if he did, was she helping or harming?

Tears started in her eyes again.

He came for me. He risked his life and came for me. He thinks I stole from him, he thinks me a thief, but he came for me. After everything I said to him...he came for me, to save me.

Her heart swelled with emotion. Emotion so strong it frightened her. Her vision was blurred, so blurred, so it was the infinitesimally slight movement of his hand that she first registered. She caught her breath, her heart squeezing. She wiped her eyes hurriedly with her free hand. The tears just welled again. But this time she saw him move, saw his eyelids lift, saw him gaze without vision for a moment and then, as if his eyes were bearing great weights, they cleared, and moved.

To her.

For a moment there was nothing in his eyes. Nothing at all.

Her heart was crushed. Just crushed.

Slowly, feeling as if a stake were being plunged into her heart, she started to draw her fingers away.

He seized them back with lightning reaction, crushing them, not letting her go.

His eyelids drooped again.

'Anna,' he said. The word was a sigh, faint and low.

His eyes sank shut.

He slid back into sleep.

But at his mouth Anna saw a faint, relaxing curve.

Later still, she was packed off back to the villa, driven by one of Leo's staff. They were all so nice to her, so kind. She wanted to shout at them, tell them it was her fault—all her fault. But the maids bore her off, got her under a shower, fed her and put her to bed.

But not in her own bed. In Leo's.

She slept, hugging his pillow.

It had his scent on it.

And her tears.

When she arrived back at the hospital it was to learn that Leo had already surfaced into full consciousness, then gone back to sleep again. His vital signs were good, his natural physical strength boosting his body's healing powers.

'He'll wake again quite soon,' the nurse told her. 'You make sure you're there when he does. And don't cry, dear. He's going to be fine, you know.'

The admonition was in vain. Anna took one look at Leo's sleeping form, his pale face, his bandaged chest, and started crying again.

Emotion filled her. Filled her and filled her. Welling up and spilling over—just like her tears.

Her heart squeezed.

Oh, Leo, she cried silently. *Leo!*

She sat down, trembling beside him, and gazed at him, her lips murmuring endlessly.

Eyes anguished.

Heart fuller than it had ever been in her life.

Full with love for Leo Makarios.

Leo was dreaming. He knew he was dreaming, because Anna was crying. She was crying, and saying she was sorry—so sorry, so sorry.

So it must be a dream.

Anna never said sorry.

She stole his Levantsky rubies, and she never said sorry.

She got him achingly aroused and then threw him out of her bedroom, and she never said sorry.

She shouted *harassment* at him, and never said sorry.

She accused him of criminal blackmail, and she never said sorry.

She called sex with him sordid, and never said sorry.

Worst of all, she got herself abducted by psychos and he had to go after her and save her and get shot to pieces.

But she was saying sorry now. He could hear her.

His eyes opened.

It wasn't a dream.

Anna Delane was sitting by his bed, her face blotched with crying, and she was saying, 'I'm sorry, Leo. I'm just so sorry.'

Then she saw his eyes open, and fell silent in mid 'sorry'.

For one long, endless moment he saw her mouth quiver, as though she were trying to control something.

Then she burst into renewed noisy tears.

Leo just stared.

Her green eyes were smeared, lashes clogged, cheeks runnelled, colour blotchy, and her nose was red.

She looked awful.

She looked the most precious sight in the world to him.

He reached for her hand. It was twisting with her other hand in her lap. There was a soggy wet tissue in their clutch. He dropped it disgustedly on the floor and took her hand, lifting it back on the bed. It felt ludicrously heavy.

But it felt the most precious thing in the world to him.

He was insane, he knew. She was a thief, a hypocrite, a cussed, unrepentant, shameless, uncooperating, accusatory damn woman, with more attitude than Genghis Khan, and she could make him angrier than he'd ever felt about a woman before. But when he'd seen her standing there, forcibly stripped to the waist, that scum jamming a gun under her ear, he'd felt a rage that he had never known in his life.

No one, *no one* was going to do that to her and live.

Even if it meant he ended up like a damn sieve, full of bullet holes!

With supreme effort he yanked her hand closer to him, possessively.

'*Theos*, but you're trouble, *yineka mou*,' he said, his voice slurring with tiredness.

Her storm of weeping increased. He watched with heavy-lidded eyes he could hardly keep open.

Well, he thought wonderingly, you see something new every day. Anna Delane, crying. His beautiful Anna, crying.

He squeezed her fingers. He wanted to haul her down on him and hold her so tight she'd never storm off again—ever. But he hadn't got the strength right now. So he just squeezed her fingers instead.

It made her cry more.

'Oh, God, Leo, I'm so sorry. I'm so sorry. It's my fault. All my fault.'

He hazed a faint smile. Anna Delane, apologising at last. It was a good feeling.

Irrelevant now, but still good.

'You came after me. You thought me a thief, and I said all those horrible things to you, and you still came after me. You saved my life—and I'm so sorry. I'm so sorry. And I'm so glad, so incredibly grateful, that you're alive.'

Leo went on watching her. He still couldn't get over hard-boiled Anna Delane bawling her eyes out for him.

It was doing the strangest thing to him. The damnedest thing.

He decided to hell with his stitches, and yanked her down to him.

It cut the apologising out instantly.

'Leo! Oh, my God—your wounds.'

She was trying to struggle up from where he'd pulled her to him. He wasn't having that. He definitely wasn't having that. She wasn't getting away from him.

'Hold still. I'm not letting you go.'

'But I'm hurting you!'

'Quiet,' ordered Leo.

He lifted his free hand and brought it round to cup her cheek. His thumb grazed her tear-wet cheek.

'Tears for me?' he said wonderingly. 'Anna Delane, crying over me?'

'Of *course* I'm crying! I owe you my *life*,' she wailed. 'And you nearly got *killed* for my sake. You nearly got killed. And I feel so *bad*. I thought you were just a spoilt, arrogant bastard who believed he could help himself to me because I was a model, that you just wanted a quick lay because you thought I was cheap and easy—and then you got sex from me by threatening me with jail, because I had to let you think I was a thief, and you didn't see *anything* wrong with getting sex that way, and I hated you for that, and I hated you even more because you made me forget that was why you were having sex with me, and that made me even angrier with you—that you could make me so *stupid* over you, wanting a man who was treating me like that—and so I hated you even more, and I was horrible to you—as horrible as I could be—and then you went and came after me when those sicko goons got me, and they would have killed me, and tortured me and you saved me and nearly got killed—you nearly got *killed*—and I thought you were dead. Oh, God, I thought you were dead, Leo, and it was… It just made everything else seem pointless and stupid, and I didn't care if you were spoilt and arrogant, because I just wanted you to be alive. I just desperately, desperately wanted you to be alive…'

Her voice choked off.

'I just wanted you to be alive,' Anna whispered. 'And I'm sorry—so sorry, Leo.'

Leo was staring at her. He'd stopped listening to her saying sorry because the novelty was over—now she was just getting in a state. Besides, it was out of character for Anna. Something else she'd said, however, was not. He forced his gradually un-fogging brain to remember what it was.

Then it came to him.

'What do you mean, spoilt and arrogant?' he demanded.

She stopped apologising abruptly.

'Well, you are. You turned up in my room in your Schloss and just thought you could help yourself.'

Leo's eyes darkened. 'You'd been inviting me all evening!'

She pulled back, jerking her hand free.

'I had *not*!'

'Good God, do you think I can't tell when a woman lights up for me?' Leo demanded.

'Well, that can't be hard—considering they all do!' she snapped.

His heavy eyes drooped. 'Not like you, they don't, Anna Delane. No woman has ever lit up for me the way you do. No woman ever will. You made me so angry,' he said contempla-tively, looking at her from his weary pose against the pillows. 'Denying what was happening. I thought you a hypocrite. When I caught you with the bracelet I was almost glad, you know. Furious, but glad.' His eyes drooped even more. 'It gave me the leverage I needed.'

'Gave you the chance to blackmail me into bed!' she flashed back.

'Well, I wasn't going to let you go to jail, was I?' he riposted. 'Not when I wanted you so much. And when I knew, *knew* you wanted me too. Whatever you said or did! And you did want me, Anna. You wanted me every night, every time.'

She jumped to her feet. How could he make her so angry, so fast?

'You didn't give me any *choice*!' she exclaimed seethingly.

'No,' he said smugly. 'I didn't, did I? But—' his expression changed '—I could never get you to purr out of bed. You wouldn't, would you, Anna Delane?' He sighed. 'You're a hard case, *yineka mou*, and if I had any sense at all I'd send you packing on the first plane back to London. Coach class,' he said darkly. His voice changed again. 'But I'm damned if I got myself shot full of holes just to lose you now. Not when I've finally got you being nice to me. And, speaking of being shot full of holes…' Yet again his voice changed, hardened, his eyes flashing—the familiar, imperious Leo. 'I need the truth about the bracelet, Anna—the police will want to talk to both of us, and if my security chief doesn't have a full dossier on your abductors by the time I get out of here he'll be looking for a new job!'

There was no baiting tone in his voice now—it was grim and bleak.

Anna opened her mouth, then closed it again.

She owed Leo the truth. He'd risked his life for her.

But she had to protect Jenny. More than ever now, she had to protect her. But she wanted to tell him the truth so much.

He saw her face working and pressed on.

'Anna—I'm not going to press charges about the bracelet. I got it back—and I got you back. But are you involved in other criminal activities? Are you involved with the likes of the scum who took you and damn near killed you? I need to know.'

The harsh edge in his voice showed her he wanted answers. Yet what he had said had made her expression lighten.

'Do you mean that?' There was an eagerness in her voice that took him aback. 'You won't press charges about the bracelet?'

His eyes narrowed again. 'Yes. Why?'

'Do you promise, Leo? Do you?'

'I just told you—'

Anna took a deep breath.

'It wasn't me who took the bracelet!'

Leo looked at her measuringly. If she had not had the truth to protect her a frisson of fear would have gone through her. His voice was harsh when he spoke.

'Anna, I caught you red-handed—'

She shook her head. Surely, after nearly losing his own life, he would see what had driven Jenny to theft? Dear God, even *she* had not thought Khalil that vicious, sending in rabid, murdering gunmen like that to find her.

She swallowed.

'You caught me trying to *return* the bracelet, not stealing it,' she said. 'But the place was swarming, so I had to keep walking. I was trying to think what to do, where I could leave it so it wouldn't point any finger of suspicion at—'

She fell silent again.

'At…?' prompted Leo. His voice was quiet, dangerously quiet.

She took a breath.

'At Jenny.'

Leo looked at her blankly.

'Jenny?'

'The blonde model; the skinny one!' said Anna, with some of her old asperity.

'That one? The neurotic-looking one? Are you telling me *she* stole the bracelet?' Leo demanded.

'Yes. She took it when the jewels spilt on the floor. She must have slipped it inside her shoe to get it into the changing room. I found her with it in her bedroom and made her see sense! I said I'd get it back and no one would know! But—but you caught me. Red-handed.'

She fell silent, biting her lip.

Emotions were working inside Leo. Strange, strong emotions. He was having difficulty controlling them. But he had to. It was essential that he did.

In his head, the world was turning upside down.

'You never stole the bracelet? You were covering for the other model?' His voice was flat.

Anna nodded dumbly.

'And you took the rap for it.' His eyes flashed suddenly. 'My God, you let me go on thinking you a thief,' he said wrathfully.

'I had to!' Anna cried. 'I couldn't let Jenny be blamed. Oh, God, Leo, she's in so much trouble already.'

'She makes a habit of stealing?' jibed Leo harshly. He seemed angry—far angrier than Anna had thought he would be when she told him the truth.

'No! I told you—she was desperate, terrified. It was just an impulse thing—opportunistic. Oh, God, Leo, she needs money to hide—and even I didn't know just how badly she needs to hide. Those gunmen weren't after me—they were after *her*. They thought I knew where she was—I told them I didn't know, but they didn't believe me. They were going to torture me to make me talk. And if they find her they'll—'

Her voice broke off, high with fright.

'Why are they after her?' Leo's voice was grim.

Anna took a sharp, painful inhalation of breath.

'She had an affair with some rich sheikh. I warned her not to. I warned her. But the idiot just went ahead anyway—and now he's trying to find her. So she's got to go into hiding. I know it sounds insane, but it's true, Leo. Look—she's *right* to be terrified. Those gunmen were killers.'

He was just lying there, looking at her. His eyes were still dark with anger.

'Leo.' She bit her lip. 'Please, *please* don't be angry—she isn't really a thief. Not really. She was just so frightened—'

'I'm not angry with Jenny,' he said in a flat voice.

She looked at him anxiously.

'If you're angry with me, I accept it. I lied to you, and covered up the truth. And I'm sorry—I really, really am. But I had to protect Jenny—'

A burst of staccato Greek came from Leo. His dark eyes glittered.

'*Christos*, it's *me* I'm angry with. For being stupid enough to let you get away with fooling me that you were a thief. I was so convinced about you. It tied in with everything I thought about you. Oh, God, Anna, it made me such a brute to you—I can't bear to think of it. And all the time—'

Remorse and guilt shot through his eyes. 'And even when I thought the worst you were getting to me. I kept thinking it was just sex, but it was so much more—so much more. And that day we spent together, when you were nice to me—oh, God, that really started to open my eyes to what was happening to me. And then you turned me down again, as if I were nothing to you—nothing at all. I was so angry with you—angry that you were calling me things I knew were true about me and didn't want to hear! Then, when I heard you'd been abducted…'

He fell silent, and she saw remembered fear stark in his eyes.

Then they flashed again. But something in them seemed lighter. Brighter. 'Damn you, Anna Delane. What I've gone through for you. I had you pegged as a troublemaker—and you are.'

'What do you mean, a troublemaker?' she demanded indignantly.

His eyes were glinting. The harshness had gone, quite gone.

'Oh, you're a troublemaker, all right, Anna Delane. I knew that from the first moment I saw you, lashing out at that jerk Embrutti. Quoting your contract at him. And it went on, didn't it? Thinking you knew better than me about not wearing all the damn Levantsky diamonds at once. Let alone not even *caring* that they were the Levantsky diamonds. And as for your *pièce de reśistance*—turning virtuous on me at the last possible moment and slinging me out of your room as if I were some kind of animal in rut. *Thee mou*, what do you call that except a troublemaker?'

She bridled. 'Just because I stand up for myself you call me a troublemaker? That is just so bloody typical! I said you were spoilt and arrogant, but I let you off lightly. You're the most—'

But what he was the most Leo never heard. Because he simply grabbed her hand, hauled her down against him, and kissed her.

It silenced her completely.

For a considerable length of time.

And when, at length, Leo released her, he cupped her cheek.

'Once a month,' he said to her, gazing into her eyes, which were not flashing or glinting now, but simply glowing with a light that had never been in them in her life before, 'on a Friday evening, for one hour, *yineka mou*, you can yell insults at me. For the rest of the time…' he brushed her mouth caressingly with his '…you purr. You purr for me, Anna Delane, because I am the only man who can make you purr, and you are so very, very good at it. You'll purr for me in bed and out, and you will be very, very happy. And so will I,' he added.

She tried to pull away, but he wouldn't let her. She didn't try again. It might hurt his wounds. Wounds he had taken for her sake—to save her life.

So she just lay there in the crook of his arm.

It felt a good place to be.

A very good place.

'You see,' he said, smoothing her hair, 'you're doing it already—aren't you, *yineka mou*. Purring away in my arms.'

She eyeballed him suspiciously. 'What's *yineka mou* mean? Troublemaker in Greek?' she demanded.

He gave a wry smile, his eyes softening.

'Truer than you know, Anna Delane. It means *my woman*— and you *are* my woman. For the rest of our lives you are going to look after me, and cosset me, and do everything you can to please me and— Ouch!' He looked at her, outrage in his face. 'I took bullets for you, woman. And, besides, I hadn't finished.'

He laid a hand against her cheek, gazing into her green, green eyes. 'For the rest of our lives I am going to look after you and keep you safe—from psycho gunmen, from anything and everything—and I'm going to cosset you and cherish you and take care of you and buy you everything I want to buy you—including cups of coffee, and all the jewellery you don't want—and I'm going to do everything I can to please you and—'

He broke off, eyeing her again sternly.

'Why does the prospect of that reduce you to tears?'

It was hard to explain to a man who asked stupid questions, so Anna didn't. She just went on crying.

Leo's arm tightened around her.

'You're getting my bandages wet,' he complained.

She went on sobbing.

There was a low knock on the door, and then it opened. The doctor standing on the threshold stopped. Anna jerked upright, face swollen, eyes bleary, nose running.

'*Tsk, tsk,* I told her you needed to see a beautiful face when you surfaced,' the doctor told Leo, shaking his head.

'I know,' agreed Leo. 'She looks awful, doesn't she? Fortunately, I love her, and she loves me, so it's all right.' He looked back at Anna. 'You do love me, don't you, *yineka mou*?' he asked conversationally.

'Yes!' wailed Anna, and burst into tears again.

EPILOGUE

'WHAT would you say to having our wedding right here on the island?' Leo asked Anna as they walked along the beach towards the villa, barefoot in the silvery sand.

He'd been out of hospital for a week now, and though his gait was slower than normal he was well on the way to a full recovery. And every day, and every night, Anna gave thanks to all the powers that be for his safety. She loved him so much she thought her heart would overflow and burst. She cherished him and fussed over him and cosseted him.

It was a daily miracle to her that he had forgiven her for nearly getting him killed, for lying to him about having stolen the rubies, for having so stupidly, idiotically, kept on denying that he had only to touch her to melt every bone in her body. And he kept feeling so bad about the way he had treated her when he'd thought her a thief—so completely different from the way he was treating her now. Cosseting her as if she were made of porcelain. Cherishing her and fussing over her, day and night, all the time. Desperate to undo the way he'd treated her.

But now, as he spoke about a wedding, she halted, staring at him.

'Wedding?' she echoed.

'It's the usual way to get married,' he said.

'Married?' she echoed again. She swallowed. 'I—I didn't know you were thinking of marrying me.'

It was his turn to stare. 'You have some objection?' he posed. She could hear the slightest, just the slightest, edge in his voice.

Her expression was troubled. 'Leo, I know what you think

182

about women wanting to marry rich men—you think they're gold-diggers, trying to trap them.'

This time it was her voice that had an edge in it.

'*Thee mou*, of course I don't think that of you! No gold-digger gives a man as hard a time as you gave me!' He shook his head in sorry memory. 'So, any more objections, *matias mou*?'

But her expression stayed troubled, despite the lightness of his tone.

'Leo—we come from very different worlds. I was brought up in a two-up, two-down next to the gasworks. Whereas you—'

He placed his hands on her shoulders. 'So now you think me a snob, do you?' He sighed. 'Anna, my family fled Turkey in the 1920s with nothing. They lived in the slums of Athens for years. It was my late grandfather and my father who made the Makarios fortune—it's all new money.'

'But there's so *much* of it!' she wailed. 'And you keep making more!'

He gave a laugh and dropped his hands.

'Anna Delane, you're the only woman I know who'd worry about that.' He replaced his hands on her shoulders and looked at her, the expression in his eyes serious now. 'If you're worried I'm going to be the kind of husband who spends all his time in the office, obsessed with making money, you couldn't be more wrong.' His dark eyes searched hers. 'I've got enough, more than enough, for the rest of my life—and for our children and their children. I want to be there for my children—our children—as my parents were not for me. So I'm not wasting any more of my life getting and spending—I've got two holes in my chest to remind me that life isn't for ever.'

Anna clutched at his arms, her eyes stricken.

'Oh, God, Leo. I'm so sorry for—'

He placed a hand over her mouth.

'I cannot believe,' he told her, 'that I used to have fantasies about you saying sorry to me. It's the biggest bore in the world!'

She flushed and pushed his hand away.

'But it's all my fault that you—'

He lowered his mouth and kissed her.

'There's just no stopping you, is there?' he asked rhetorically.

'No,' she said.

And kissed him back.

Then, reluctantly, she drew away.

'Leo, I still don't think you should marry me. We could just—well, you know.'

'Live in sin?' His voice was wryly caustic.

'Yes. You see…' She gazed up at him earnestly, her eyes troubled. 'None of this was meant to happen, was it? You only really wanted a night with me—maybe one or two, whatever else any other woman you went after got. It was only because you wanted your pound of flesh after the stupid rubies, and then all that nightmare with the gunmen, and you nearly dying, and—well, all that stuff. Otherwise it would have been over ages ago. I think we're really still in post-traumatic shock— well, you mainly, I guess—and it's making you a bit doolalley. Thinking about weddings and stuff like that. If you waited a few weeks you'd be back to normal again, I'm sure.'

Leo had taken a step backwards. An expression of outrage was gathering strength on his features.

'I have taken,' he said grimly, 'everything I am going to take from you, Anna Delane. You have been absolutely nothing but trouble since I laid eyes on you. But this—this is too much. You actually dare to stand there and look me in the eyes and tell me I must be insane to want to marry you. Good God, woman,' he roared, 'I love you! Do you understand? Yes, I was a fool, a total idiot, thinking it was just sex I wanted. But I've wised up now. It took a couple of bullets to wise me up, but I have. And so have you. Now we both know it's love, not just sex. So from now on that's what we both do. *Love each other.* For ever. All our lives. You see that sun out there, Anna Delane? It shines out of me. Understand? You'd better because I can tell you it damn well shines out of you. Now—' he heaved a big breath '—I don't want to hear any more of this. Understand?'

'Yes, but I—'

He silenced her with a kiss.

'Stop arguing,' he told her.

'But I—'

'Stop—' he kissed her '—arguing.'

When she surfaced, after a long, long time, she gazed up at him. He was right, damn it, she thought.

The sun really did shine out of him. It was infuriating. But it was true.

He read her expression, eyes twining with hers.

'It's the same for me, Anna,' he told her softly. 'It really, really is.'

She went on gazing up at him adoringly.

Leo let her do it, and did it back, because he was helpless, quite helpless to do otherwise—all his life. For ever.

A stray memory flickered in his brain. The redhead at the Schloss, gazing adoringly up at his cousin. Markos ought to marry her, he thought. He must remember to tell him so. He would lend the girl the Levantsky emeralds for her wedding day.

And speaking of the Levantsky jewels...

'Don't move.'

'I can't anyway!'

'Good.'

Leo stood back, surveying his handiwork.

'Two last pieces.'

He dipped his hand into the almost empty crystal bowl. He picked up a pair of sapphire earrings and carefully arranged them symmetrically.

Then he surveyed his handiwork once more.

'Perfect,' he said.

He reached for the camera.

'Are you sure? I don't want anything showing that shouldn't!'

'You have my word.'

'OK—well, go on, then. Get it over and done with!'

Leo looked disapprovingly down at her.

'You really have no soul, have you?'

'I've got a stiff back, an itch behind my knee, a clasp is sticking into me somewhere sensitive, and if I sneeze, Leo Makarios, you are going to have a roomful of flying jewellery!'

'Don't even think of it, Kyria Makarios,' he said, and started snapping.

'I must be mad,' muttered Leo's brand-new wife.

'Just besotted,' said Anna's brand-new husband.

He clicked away again.

'OK, darling—give me sexy!' he instructed.

'Stuff off,' growled Anna.

'Pouting and sulky—just as good,' returned Leo.

'You're a pervert, you know that? Taking photos like this!'

'It's a one-off private art show, my beloved. Indulge me. You'll never let me do this again, will you?'

'Too damn right,' she growled.

He lowered his camera.

'Anna—if you could see yourself now you would understand. You simply look—unbelievable.'

His eyes swept over her lying in his bed, her naked body covered in jewels.

He lifted his hand helplessly.

'You outshine every one of them,' he said softly. 'And all of them together.'

'They're just crystals, Leo.'

He looked down at her, at her glittering rainbow body.

'And you are just a woman—but you are *my* woman, the most precious in the world to me. And if I lost you my life would end.'

Slowly, he raised the camera, and took one last picture.

Then he put the camera aside and came towards her.

'And do you know the best, the very best, part of this, my adored bride on her wedding night? This,' he told her.

Carefully he lifted up a diamond ring from her navel and slipped it inside the crystal bowl.

'This,' he said, and removed a sapphire collar from where it lay around her arm.

'This,' he said, lifting a ruby tiara from where it circled her left breast.

It took him a long, long time to remove them all.

Until at last only the necklace of diamonds was left, cascading from her throat.

'That stays,' said Leo.

He bent over to kiss her, long and languorously.

Anna's eyes gleamed. 'Don't you want me to wear the whole *parure*?' she asked.

Leo frowned disapprovingly. 'That would be vulgar,' he told her loftily.

Her mouth pressed together. 'Leo Makarios, you are the most—'

'I know.' He smiled with insufferable self-satisfaction, and grazed one bare, beautiful breast with his velvet lips. 'The most irresistible man you've ever met.'

Anna locked her arms around his neck and dragged him down to her. 'Yes! Damn it!' she said.

e◆HARLEQUIN.com

The Ultimate Destination for Women's Fiction

Calling all aspiring writers!
Learn to craft the perfect romance novel
with our useful tips and tools:

- Take advantage of our **Romance Novel
  Critique Service** for detailed advice from
  romance professionals.

- Use our **message boards** to connect with
  writers, published authors and editors.

- Enter our **Writing Round Robin—**
  you could be published online!

- Learn many tools of the writer's trade
  from editors and authors in our
  On Writing section!

- **Writing guidelines** for Harlequin or
  Silhouette novels—what our editors
  really look for.

Learn more about romance writing
from the experts—

visit www.eHarlequin.com today!

INTLTW04R

MODELS &
MILLIONAIRES

**Escape to a world of absolute
wealth, glamour and romance…**

In this brand-new duet from Julia James,
models find themselves surrounded by beauty
and sophistication. It can be a false world, but
fortunately there are strong alpha millionaires
waiting in the wings to claim them!

On sale this May,

Markos Makarios thinks Vanessa is the best
mistress he has ever had—until he has to
warn her not to think of marriage.
Mistresses are only for pleasure, after all….

FOR PLEASURE…
OR MARRIAGE?
by Julia James

Get your copy today!

www.eHarlequin.com   HPMM0506

If you enjoyed what you just read,
then we've got an offer you can't resist!

Take 2 bestselling
love stories FREE!
Plus get a FREE surprise gift!

Clip this page and mail it to Harlequin Reader Service®

IN U.S.A.	IN CANADA
3010 Walden Ave.	P.O. Box 609
P.O. Box 1867	Fort Erie, Ontario
Buffalo, N.Y. 14240-1867	L2A 5X3

YES! Please send me 2 free Harlequin Presents® novels and my free surprise gift. After receiving them, if I don't wish to receive anymore, I can return the shipping statement marked cancel. If I don't cancel, I will receive 6 brand-new novels every month, before they're available in stores! In the U.S.A., bill me at the bargain price of $3.80 plus 25¢ shipping & handling per book and applicable sales tax, if any*. In Canada, bill me at the bargain price of $4.47 plus 25¢ shipping & handling per book and applicable taxes**. That's the complete price and a savings of at least 10% off the cover prices—what a great deal! I understand that accepting the 2 free books and gift places me under no obligation ever to buy any books. I can always return a shipment and cancel at any time. Even if I never buy another book from Harlequin, the 2 free books and gift are mine to keep forever.

106 HDN DZ7Y
306 HDN DZ7Z

Name	(PLEASE PRINT)	
Address	Apt.#	
City	State/Prov.	Zip/Postal Code

Not valid to current Harlequin Presents® subscribers.

Want to try two free books from another series?
Call 1-800-873-8635 or visit www.morefreebooks.com.

* Terms and prices subject to change without notice. Sales tax applicable in N.Y.
** Canadian residents will be charged applicable provincial taxes and GST.
 All orders subject to approval. Offer limited to one per household.
® are registered trademarks owned and used by the trademark owner or its licensee.

PRES04R   ©2004 Harlequin Enterprises Limited

HARLEQUIN *Presents*~

Surrender to seduction under a golden sun

Why not relax and let Harlequin Presents® whisk you
away to stunning international locations where irresistible
men and sophisticated women fall in love....

Don't miss this opportunity to experience glamorous
lifestyles and exotic settings!

This month...

Cesare Saracino wants revenge on the thief
who stole from his family! But the woman
he forces back to Italy is the thief's identical twin,
Milly Lee. Then desire flares between them....

THE ITALIAN'S PRICE

by Diana Hamilton

on sale May 2006

www.eHarlequin.com

HPFA0506

UNcut

Even more passion for your reading pleasure!

You'll find the drama, the emotion, the international
settings and the happy endings that you love
in Harlequin Presents. But we've turned up the
thermostat a little, so that the relationships really
sizzle.... Careful, they're almost too hot to handle!

Are you ready?

"Captive in His Bed weaves together romance,
passion, action adventure and espionage into
one thrilling story that will keep you turning the
pages…Sandra Marton does not disappoint."
—Shannon Short, *Romantic Times BOOKclub*

CAPTIVE IN HIS BED
by Sandra Marton

on sale May 2006

*Look out for the next thrilling
Knight brothers story, coming in July!*

www.eHarlequin.com

HPUC0506